PULGA

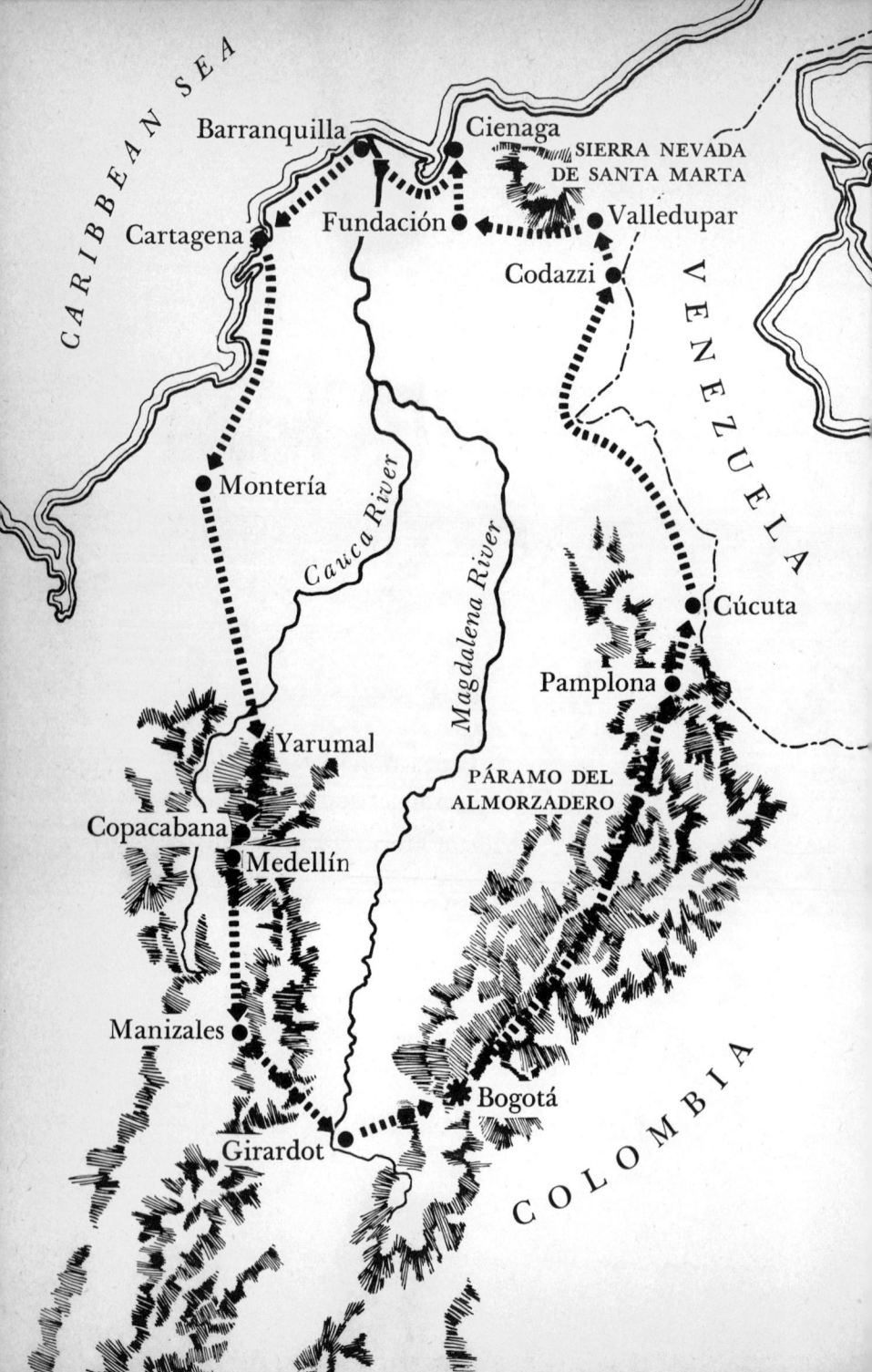

PULGA

BY S. R. VAN ITERSON

Translation from the Dutch
by Alexander and Alison Gode

William Morrow and Company
New York

In writing this book I am greatly indebted to Don Daniel Olarte, manager of a large shipping firm. The names and descriptions of persons and estates are fictitious. Any resemblance to real persons and places is coincidental.

Translation copyright © 1971 by William Morrow and Company, Inc. Original Dutch language edition published by Uitgeverij Leopold, The Hague, Holland, under the title *De Adjudant van de Vrachtwagen*, © Uitgeverij Leopold, The Hague, Holland. All rights reserved. No part of this book may be reproduced or utilized in any form or by any means, electronic or mechanical, including photocopying, recording or by any information storage and retrieval system, without permission in writing from the Publisher. Inquiries should be addressed to William Morrow and Company, Inc., 105 Madison Ave., New York, N.Y. 10016. Printed in the United States of America. Library of Congress Catalog Card Number: 77-143462
1 2 3 4 5 75 74 73 72 71

CONTENTS

1	The Boy from Midtown	9
2	The House in the North	20
3	Gilimon Naranjo	28
4	Mamá Maruja's Place	
	Bogotá to Cúcuta	39
5	To the Páramo del Almorzadero	51
6	The Encounter at the Coffee Shop	61
7	The House on the Río Seco	67
8	The Prophecy of the Old Woman	77
9	Driving Down to the Coast	
	Cúcuta to Barranquilla	88

10	Eduardo	97
11	On to Fundación	107
12	The Ferry Across the Magdalena River	118
13	Pulga's Tennis Shoes	127
14	Jaime's Family Barranquilla to Copacabana	134
15	The Wake for Menardo	145
16	Loading Cattle	155
17	The Storytellers	168
18	The Trunk of the Devil Copacabana to Bogotá	177
19	The Hacienda La Virginia	189
20	The Hut of the Terrible Death	197
21	Pulga's Story	204
22	The Accident	216
23	Homecoming	229

This book is for all of you:
Foyita, Victor, Loretta, Marnix,
and for Colombia, a great and inspiring country,
which you have been privileged to know.
S. R. VAN ITERSON

We dedicate this translation
to Frederick J. Briccetti, M.D.,
without whom it would not be.
ALEXANDER AND ALISON GODE

1

THE BOY FROM MIDTOWN

The sun was going down, and right away the air became quite cold. Gray clouds settled over the Andes. It began to rain, a penetrating, cold drizzle.

Pulga, shivering in his threadbare clothes, stood in the big market area in the center of town. Rain pattered on the bundles of onions, baskets of tomatoes, bunches of green bananas. Water trickled down through the piles of oranges, carrots, pineapples, lettuce, melons, peas, papayas, tangerines, cucumbers, and mangoes on the ground. The unpaved streets were a sea of mud.

PULGA

Huddled in their black wraps, the women sat among wet sacks of potatoes and cassava, crates of eggs, tied-up chickens, and heaps of dripping vegetables and fruits. Slowly some of them started to pack their things. Others pulled a piece of burlap or a sheet of plastic over their heads and just sat there, babies pressed closely under their shawls. A child in a tomato basket was crying. Bigger children, numb with cold, men's dark hats pulled down over their bluish faces, were sitting clustered together among piles of refuse.

Pulga looked around. For quite a while he had been keeping an eye on a parked car, hoping to get a tip from the driver for watching it while he was gone. But he was out of luck. The driver was taking his time.

Pulga's eyes wandered over the stalls, set up along the row of houses, where chunks of meat were roasting over charcoal fires. Thick, white sausages lay in enamel tubs, and pig's skin was frying in oil. Pots full of potatoes boiled in their jackets stood on the ground.

Pulga was ravenously hungry, and his mouth watered. Casually he walked over to the nearest stall. But the woman, constantly wiping her greasy fingers on her bulging apron, kept a steady eye on him.

It was dark now and raining harder. Gradually

The Boy from Midtown

the market area became deserted. Women and children pulled their little flat carts with unsold vegetables into the small side streets and disappeared in the darkness. Men came to sweep the refuse into heaps.

The car Pulga had been watching was gone. He felt annoyed. With his bare foot he kicked a rotten orange, turned around, and trotted off. The narrow streets in the center of town were bustling. It was the time of day when the offices closed, and crowds of people were waiting at bus stops or looking at displays in lighted shop windows. Automobile horns kept tooting. Newsboys were shouting: "Extra! Extra! Another raid in Tolima!"

In some streets the first Christmas decorations were already up. Out of a brightly lit shop came a sturdy boy with two little girls in blue woolen coats. The collar of the boy's sports jacket was turned up and his hands were thrust deep into his pockets.

"Did you hear, Jorge Gabriel," the older girl said. "Another raid in Tolima. Could that be near our hacienda?"

The boy laughed condescendingly. "Of course not, child. What are you thinking of! There are so many workmen at La Virginia, the bandits know better than to set foot on our land!"

"Can you hold my doll for me, Jorge Gabriel?" asked the younger girl. She held up the big doll with blond curls and a tulle dress that she just had been given.

"There's our car now. Hurry, Beatriz," directed the boy. "Come, Ana María."

The chauffeur opened the door of the Mercedes, and the three children got in. The car rolled away. Pulga, who had latched onto the back of the car, rolled away with it.

"Oh, look! There is someone hanging on the back of our car!" Beatriz called out, rather annoyed. She was kneeling on the back seat, her nose close to the rear window. "Jorge Gabriel, Ana María, just look!"

Ana María was too busy with her doll, but Jorge Gabriel looked around, straight into Pulga's grimy face. His first reaction was to chase the boy off the car. Then he realized that would not do much good. He pulled Beatriz away from the window and made her sit down next to him.

"Just one of those street urchins," he said shortly. "Don't bother about him."

Slowly the Mercedes drove on for several blocks, and Pulga jumped off, slipped through the lines of cars, and disappeared into a narrow, sloping side street in the old part of town. Here there were no tall modern buildings with rows of lighted windows aligned like the eyes of huge pineapples rising up into the dark sky, no glittering window displays, no brilliant neon signs.

The houses were low; behind the iron-barred windows the shutters were closed. The badly paved, narrow streets smelled of garbage. At some street corners there were shabby stores without windows. Light shone through open doors into the street.

Pulga stopped in front of one of the large dark buildings, which had a double iron-studded door with a hinged panel standing ajar. He stepped inside onto a wide, moist, cobbled passageway leading to an inner patio. From there a narrower passage led to a second court, beyond which was a neglected grass plot with an untended fig tree. Around the patios were the living quarters, the kitchens, stables, and outbuildings of a huge old house, where long ago one of the first families of Bogotá had lived. Now every room was occupied by a whole family. Most of the families had many children and sometimes included relatives.

Some of the doors stood open, and a diffused light fell on the wet, shining stones of the patio. Out of the semi-darkness rose a confusion of sounds—the shrieking of women, the crying of children, rough voices of men, the blaring of radios. A man came stumbling down shaky wooden steps. A woman was yelling, "Liar, scoundrel, lazy bum ... with my hard-earned pennies!" Little boys were playing in the rain, hitting the water that came gushing out of a broken rainspout with sticks.

In one room a woman stood at a table, ironing. Next to her on the floor was a basket of fine wash, which she would deliver the following day to one of the great houses in the north. A flock of children played on the floor. The oldest girl sat in the doorway trying to hush the baby.

In the dimly lit room of Rose-Alba a sewing machine hummed. Under the stairs an old man was shining shoes. His little boy and his bottle of *aguardiente* were next to him.

Joaquin the half-wit was busy, by the light of a candle, clipping streamers from sheets of colored paper. Streamers lay everywhere, on the dirty bed, the table, the rotted wooden floor. They hung over the back of the chair, the pot of food, against the dirty plaster walls.

Pulga walked across the large patio, through the narrow passageway to the inner court. Long ago this had been the servants' quarters. A woman stood washing at the big stone trough. Eulalia-with-the-Ear, a doddering old woman with only one ear, sat in her room, formerly one of the storerooms of the house, the *despensa de dulce*. Some of the shelves where pots and bottles of sweets had been kept were still attached to the wall. At the coal stove in the smoke-blackened kitchen two women were quarreling over a frying pan.

Pulga pushed open the door of the room where he lived with his grandmother, his two younger sisters, and his young brother, Pedro. His grandmother was sitting on the edge of the iron bedstead, which was covered with newspapers, feeding the little girls a grayish broth from a pot. She did not look up when Pulga came in, but kept talking and mumbling to herself. *"Dios mío, Dios mío,* Virgen Santa, life is hard, life is bitter."

Pedro was sitting in a corner on the floor. When he saw Pulga, he quickly got up and dragged himself toward him. One of his feet was badly twisted. He walked almost on his ankle.

"Look here," he said to Pulga, "look what I got." He proudly showed a faded green sweater with holes in the elbows.

"Where did you get it?"

"From Consuelo. She was here this afternoon."

"Did she bring anything else?"

Pedro shook his head. "Just a piece of *panela,* but they ate it all." He motioned with his head in the direction of the bed where their grandmother and sisters were sitting. "She just dropped in. She couldn't stay long," he added.

"What are you sitting in here for? Why aren't you playing outside with the others?"

Pedro's face fell. "Just because," he said.

"But why, what's wrong?"

"Nothing." Pedro turned his pinched little face away from his brother.

Pulga shrugged his shoulders. What could he do? Of course, they had called him Cripple again. Pedro would have to get used to it.

Outside a voice called, "Ready? Where are you hiding? Come here, for God's sake!" Suddenly all was quiet in the patio.

Pulga stepped out and peered through the small passageway toward the large courtyard. "There is Tío Pepe." He looked at his little brother, at his shriveled face, at the twisted foot, and he saw a shiver run through the thin body in the faded sweater that was too large.

Tío Pepe shuffled along slowly in the direction of the inner patio, followed by his wife and children. The tapping of his cane sounded hollow through the passageway. In the middle of the patio he stopped, tapping his cane on the ground. Water squirted up between the loose bricks.

"Where are you hiding?" he called out again.

With half-closed eyes Tío Pepe looked at Pulga. "Where is that brother of yours?"

A sudden impulse made Pulga say, "I will come along tonight."

"You? Not on a bet. It is Pedro I want. He brings

in money with that paw of his. Pedro! Where the Devil...!"

Pedro dragged himself outside past Pulga.

"Is that all of us now?" Tío Pepe looked around. "Take off that sweater, boy. A dressed-up gentleman does me no good. Have you got the child?"

His wife, with a year-old child on her arm, nodded.

The procession—Tío Pepe, his wife and nine children, including three that were borrowed—began moving. In the dark room the grandmother mumbled to herself, "Virgen Santa, Madre de Dios . . . ai . . . ai . . . ai. . . ."

Pulga followed the little group through the narrow passageway, across the large courtyard, out to the wide paved entrance. At the gate he stopped and watched them go off. Pedro was the last to straggle around the corner. The street was dark and desolate, the pavement wet and glistening. Faintly Pulga could hear the noise of traffic on the broad, business thoroughfares. Close by he also heard a whisper of voices. Two men were leaning against the wall, talking to each other. When they caught sight of Pulga, they both fell silent.

"What do you want?" asked one of them finally.

"It's me, Pulga. Is that you, Enrique?"

"Sure enough, it is Pulga," said the man, coming

closer. Then, slowly, he added, "Say, I've got an idea! Hey, Ricardo, come over here. No, you come along with me, boy."

Slowly Pulga joined the two men, who continued to whisper, pointing at him, looking him over very carefully.

"What do you think, will it work?" asked Enrique.

"Who can tell?" answered Ricardo. He kept looking at Pulga. "I think it might," he said at last.

"We can easily find out. Tell me, how old are you?" asked Enrique.

"Fourteen or fifteen," answered Pulga hesitantly.

"Fifteen?" repeated Ricardo doubtfully. "You don't look any more than ten."

Pulga said nothing.

Ricardo leaned toward him. "You're not bluffing, are you?"

Pulga still did not answer, but Enrique said, "No, it tallies more or less. We've known each other for a while, haven't we, Pulga? After all, it's not for nothing that they call you the Flea." He turned to Ricardo. "You decide, but if you ask me, this is just what we need. He's as small as they come, but old enough not to make a mess of it."

Ricardo motioned with his head, and the two men walked away. Over his shoulder Ricardo called back, "Stay here and wait for us, you hear?"

The Boy from Midtown

Pulga remained standing by the doorway. The rain had stopped, but the night air was cold. He waited for a long time. His stomach was rumbling. He thought of the gray soup his grandmother had been feeding his sisters. Would any of it be left over? Still, he did not dare leave.

Finally the two men came back. "Come with us," they said to Pulga.

2

THE HOUSE IN THE NORTH

"You can make something on it," said Enrique.

"Of course, that goes without saying," confirmed Ricardo. "Tit for tat," he snickered.

They were sitting at a table in the rear of a small coffee shop. Pulga had had a cup of black coffee and a couple of stale yucca rolls. He scarcely heard what the men were saying. He was too scared.

"What do you say?" asked Enrique, shoving another dry roll across the dirty tabletop to Pulga.

"What did you say about the dog?" asked Pulga with a full mouth.

The House in the North

"Oh, by now that dog has had it," answered Ricardo. "Didn't I tell you? I gave him a nice chunk of meat this afternoon. No stinking scraps, a nice chunk of meat. Properly dressed." He laughed. "No unfinished business."

"Did you see him eat it?" asked Enrique.

Ricardo did not answer. He gulped down what was left of his beer, set the empty bottle on the table with a bang, and got up. "So that's settled," he said, paying for the coffee, the rolls, and the beer.

When they were outside, he turned to Pulga. "So that's settled," he repeated, more emphatically. "So long. We'll see you tonight up north, where I told you. Make sure you get there on time."

The two men walked away, each in a different direction. Pulga took his time. Slowly he moved along in the direction of the brightly lit streets in midtown. The traffic was heavy, the cafés were full of people, and outside the movie houses crowds were waiting for the second show to begin.

The night air was bitter cold. People coming out from the first show covered their faces with handkerchiefs. Women sat crouched in doorways, babies under their wraps, their hands outstretched. Grimy children ran about, also begging. Pulga knew that somewhere outside one of the movie houses Tío Pepe's wife was hanging around with her little group. Her husband was watching from a distance.

Pulga knew everything that was going on around there. He knew the filthy little boys that were running around between the parked cars. They pushed one another out of the way, snarling like wild dogs, tinny voices shrieking. "I was here first! I'm watching this one!"

When he thought it was about time to go, he headed north taking the bus. Pulga's way of taking the bus was to latch onto the rear of it. Every time the bus stopped, he slid down to the ground. When it started moving, he pulled himself up on it again. The last stretch he walked.

It was quiet in this part of town, and a smell of flowers and moist earth hung in the air. The wet pavement shone under the light of street lamps. Blooming trees swayed in the night wind.

From the shadow under the trees came a "Pssst!"

Pulga quickly looked around, and then stepped into the shadow where he saw Ricardo casually leaning against a tree. "You made it in good time," he said. "Enrique will be here in a moment."

"But—" Pulga began.

"Hold your tongue! And don't you worry. Just keep your chin up," Ricardo ordered.

They waited for quite a while. Then Enrique joined them without a word. Ricardo looked at his watch. "There is no need to wait any longer," he said. They both looked at Pulga.

"Now, get going," whispered Enrique. "The upper window of the pantry. Once you're inside, you just walk across to the front door and unlatch it. We take care of the rest."

"But the . . . the dog," Pulga whispered, "and if they hear me. . . ."

"What do you mean?" snarled Enrique impatiently. "Who could hear you? I told you, didn't I? Nobody lives in the house but an old woman, just an old woman with her two servants. She can't hear a thing, and if the girls happen to hear you, they'll know better than to make a fuss, I swear. And the dog, there *is* no dog anymore. Ricardo told you about that. Don't start making things difficult, Pulga." He grabbed Pulga by his neck and pushed him down so that he could look through under the branches and see the houses on the other side.

"You see that yellow house with the iron fence around it? That's it. When you walk up the gravel path past the front door, you will see a little farther on next to the garage a small broken window. There you slip in. Then you open the front door and beat it. That's all you have to do. We take care of the rest. Tomorrow we meet near your place. You'll be well off then, I tell you."

"Well off or well under—it all depends on how you handle this thing," Ricardo said with a nasty smirk.

Pulga wiped his mouth with the back of his hand. Without a word, he stepped out of the shadow of the trees and walked up the street. Slowly he moved on in the direction of the big, yellow house.

All the curtains were drawn. Except for a small lamp over the front door, the place was dark. Quickly but carefully he stepped inside the grounds, walked across the lawn by the side of the gravel path, and turned at the corner of the building. There was the garage. His eyes glided along the wall. There was the small broken window. Indeed, it could not be called anything but small. Pulga looked all around to make certain that he was alone.

Everything was quiet in the garden. In the house next door a faint light shone through the leaded panes in the stairwell. Somewhere a door slammed. Was that in the other house? For a few moments Pulga stood stockstill. When he heard nothing more, he moved his hand along the wall.

The first five feet or so from the ground were made of quarry stone. His fingers and toes gripped it easily. He reached out over the windowsill, pulled himself up, and squeezed his shoulders through the small window. Pulga could bend and stretch his body like a cat. His groping fingers got hold of the woodwork, and he worked himself farther inside. He held onto the edge, drew himself all the way through, and silently slid down to the floor.

The House in the North

It was pitch dark. For a few moments he stood still, hardly breathing, listening. The house was silent. His eyes began to adjust to the darkness. Cautiously he groped around.

The room was small and narrow, and he remembered that Enrique—or was it Ricardo?—had said something about a pantry. He looked up at the small rectangular spot of light, which was the window. If he got caught, it would not be easy to make his escape through there. The way back was cut off.

Carefully Pulga took a few steps, his hands stretched out in front of him. There . . . that was a door. His fingers found the knob, and slowly he opened the door just a crack.

The dog . . . what was it they had said about the dog? Ricardo had poisoned him, but had he seen the dog eat the meat? Dogs in the north had more to eat than the children of the slums. Perhaps the dog had not touched Ricardo's meat. Perhaps he was lying somewhere in the dark, ready to attack. Pulga heard his heart beating. He opened the door a little wider and waited. Everything remained quiet. He moved on slowly feeling his way along the wall. Now a door, a wall, another door. No, it was the door he had come through, the door to the pantry. Somewhere he had lost his sense of direction. Taking a chance, he turned, opened the first door he came to, and stepped inside.

The floor under his feet was smooth and cold . . . tile. He smelled roast meat. Through a large window a dim light shone into the room. All around were large, white shiny objects. This was the kitchen. The front door, Enrique had said.

But where was the front door? And where did the servants sleep? Over the garage? Or next to the kitchen? And the dog . . . what had they done to the dog? Was he dead? Or was he lying and watching somewhere in this large dark house?

Step by step, Pulga made his way back to the little room he had come through. But he could not stop now. He had to go on, he had to.

Again he groped around for a door. Cautiously he turned the knob. The door was slightly jammed, and the hinges squeaked fearfully. He held the door ajar, listened, but heard nothing, nothing except the beating of his own heart.

Had he opened the door wide enough? Making himself as small as possible, he slipped through like a cat. His feet touched something soft and woolly. The dog? No, he was standing on a soft woolen rug, not an animal. The room looked narrow and long, a hallway. And there, at its end, a spot of light shone in from the burning lamp outside. Pulga breathed deeply. That was the front door. Enrique had been right, there was nothing to it. Child's play!

He took a few quick steps in the direction of the

light and bumped into a side table. Its legs scraped across the floor, and the sound echoed through the stairwell. After a moment a door opened upstairs.

An old woman's voice called out, "Is that you, María?"

Pulga stood there petrified.

"María, are you there? Is something wrong?"

He heard a creaking sound on the floor upstairs. Then a light went on.

Pulga acted without thinking. With a few quick steps he reached the front hall and found a recess containing long, heavy coats. He pressed himself against the wall behind the coats. The light from upstairs shone past him.

He heard shuffling footsteps. The wooden floor creaked. Then the light went out, and a door closed. Again silence filled the big house. Pulga kept his thin body stiff between the wall and the woolen garments and did not move for a long time.

Finally, he came out. He walked up to the front door, carefully pushed the bolt, turned the knob, and opened the door.

The light blinded him. The cold night air hit his face. For a second he stood motionless, shivering, his eyes half closed. Then he stepped out, ran across the wet lawn toward the fence, and vanished into the dark quiet street.

The front door remained open.

3

GILIMON NARANJO

There was no sign of a letup in the rainy season. Dark clouds came from the llanos over the mountains and dropped torrents of rain over the city. Hailstones bounced off the streets, piled high along the sidewalks, clogged the sewers. The streets were a mesh of dirty rivers. From the bare hills, heavy, yellowish mud, which looked like lava, oozed down. Gravel and stones were carried along into the streets of the city, stalling traffic.

Pulga stood in the doorway of the room where he lived, up to his ankles in the water. He kept staring at the rain. The hail and rubbish from the broken gutter had clogged up the drain. The patio was a vast lake, and water was running into the rooms.

Pulga's grandmother sat huddled on the bed. His two little sisters had snuggled up against her. The water in the room was five inches deep.

Pedro came along with an old broom. "I got it from Joaquin," he said, and began sweeping.

Pulga watched him for a while, then said, "It's no good. The drain is clogged. The water comes back in as fast as you sweep it out. Can't you see?"

Again he stared outside. Eulalia-with-the-Ear came out of her storeroom and waded across the inner court, her skirts dragging through the water. In a vague sort of way she looked happy. A rat swam by, heading for the higher rooms on the other side. Now and then someone came out of a room, poked around in the drain with a stick, and waded back again.

Nothing could be done. The rain kept falling out of the gray sky in buckets.

"Ave María, Virgen Santa," mumbled the old grandmother on her bed. The little girls, numb with cold, snuggled up to her still closer. Pulga pulled his head down between his shoulders, and with a few bold jumps he got across the patio to the paved passageway. Soaked to the skin, he stood by the main door looking up and down the street.

He did not really think that they would show up. A whole week had gone by since the night of the burglary in the north, and he had seen nothing of Enrique or Ricardo.

The first few days he had stayed near home, hanging around in the street. Afterward he had made the rounds of the coffee shops in the neighborhood. Enrique and Ricardo were smart enough not to appear. Pulga shrugged his shoulders. That was life. What could he do about it? In his fourteen or fifteen years—he did not know himself exactly how old he was—he had seen enough of life not to be surprised by anything.

His mother had died after the birth of his youngest sister, and then his father had stopped coming home altogether. Consuelo, his oldest sister, had found a job in another part of town. She paid the rent, and occasionally she brought something to eat or a piece of worn-out clothing. His grandmother, who had been living with them for some time, stayed on.

Of the neighbors, no one—except Tío Pepe— bothered about the family. They all had their own worries. Tío Pepe soon had taken note of Pedro. A cripple was just what he needed to bring in cash. At first he had let Pedro share the earnings, but as time went on that share had dwindled. Pedro could not stand up against Tío Pepe, and when Pulga

PULGA

his friends, "That takes care of the grease job. Tomorrow morning I'll be off again." He paid his bill and, pulling his head down between his shoulders, ran across the street to his truck.

The driver jumped into his cab, started the motor, opened the side window, and wiped the fogged windshield. Shifting into gear, he stepped slowly on the gas pedal. The wheels began to turn.

Outside, through the downpour, a voice called out, "Gilimon, hold it! Someone's underneath!"

Gilimon turned the steering wheel.

"Gilimon!"

Gilimon stuck his head out the side window. "What's wrong?"

"There's someone underneath!"

With a curse, Gilimon jumped out of the cab.

The man who had called out to him was staring under the body of the truck at the back, his hands on his knees. Several men in the coffee shop came out, leaving their drinks behind.

Gilimon bent down and dragged Pulga out from between the wheels. "What the devil . . . you brat!" he shouted.

Pulga, still half asleep, stared into Gilimon's face. Slowly he stood up and looked around to make his getaway, but Gilimon had a tight grip on his arm.

"That was a narrow escape," said the man who had warned Gilimon. With obvious satisfaction he tried to say something, there was hell to pay. That's how things were.

When the rain let up, Pulga went to the marketplace in the center of town, where he usually spent much of his time trying to earn a few pennies as a car watcher.

In this weather few cars were there to be watched. The market was a sad sight with its soaked bags, baskets, produce, and muddy paths between the stands. Women sat crouching beside their wares, water dripping from the brims of their men's hats.

Pulga ran up to a car that was about to park. "Let me watch, let me watch!" he shouted.

A man shoved him aside. Pinned to the lapel of his plastic raincoat was a round piece of cardboard on which was written: *Car Watcher.*

"Get going, boy," the man ordered, when Pulga tried to resist. He tore a slip of printed paper from a pad and shoved it under the windshield wiper. The owners of the car and a servant girl carrying baskets stepped out and disappeared into the market area.

"But . . . but this is where I always watch," said Pulga.

"You do, hey? Maybe you did!" said the car watcher. "But now I am here. Get going!" He motioned threateningly.

Pulga moved on. From a safe distance he looked back at the intruder and told him what he thought of him. Then he ran off down a side street. He tightened the string holding up the trousers that were much too big for him and walked on aimlessly, up one street, down another.

To go home where everything was underwater and where his grandmother and his sisters were crouching on the bed made no sense. There might be barely enough room for Pedro, but not for the five of them.

He kept going until he came to a street full of big trucks. The place was busy, with drivers, *ruanas* over their shoulders, walking around the vehicles, checking waybills, freight, the trucks themselves. They shouted, laughed, swore, slapped each other on the shoulder, and wandered in groups or singly back and forth between the coffee shops and their jobs.

The unceasing din of honking horns was deafening. As soon as one truck left the lineup and drove away, another arrived to fill its place. The heavy trucks were dusty and spattered, their wheels covered with mud. They had traveled thousands of miles, over poor roads, across the mountains, through the sweltering heat of the flatlands, along precipitous cliffs, through the mist and across the treeless plateaus called *páramos*.

Pulga stopped to look at one of the huge trucks. The trailer was supported by axles with enormous double wheels. He counted them one by one. There were eight of them. The red cab was shining, the headlights and the chrome bumpers were shining. The large mirrors outside the side windows were shining too. Written over the windshield were the words *Mi Amor*. The motor hummed softly. The driver was standing on the front bumper, the upper half of his body hidden under the open hood.

Pulga sneaked up to the cab. He could feel the warmth of the motor. Heavy drops were tapping again on the pavement; once more it began to pour. Within a few moments the street was deserted. The men had fled into the coffee shops. The driver, who had been standing on the bumper of his truck, closed the hood, stopped the motor, and ran to join the others.

Pulga looked around. Except for the coffee shop, where they would have chased him out anyway, there was no shelter in sight. Without a second thought, he slipped under the truck and sat down between the rear wheels. He heard the rain drumming on the canvas roof high above his head. It did not bother him now. Where he was sitting was nice and dry. He stretched out, rested his head on his hands, and looked at the raindrops, glistening in the light from the shops. His eyelids were heavy as lead. His head sank down. Pulga was asleep.

Inside the coffee shop, Gilimon Naranjo

went on his way while the others went back to their drinks.

Gilimon and Pulga faced each other in the pouring rain. "OK," said Gilimon, "what the devil did you think you were doing?"

Pulga said nothing.

"Well. . . ." said Gilimon.

"I . . . I didn't do anything," stammered Pulga. "I was asleep. I must have been asleep."

"Asleep, under my truck! What have you got a head for? Just think, those wheels of mine were ready to crush you to a pulp. Why don't you go home to sleep?"

Pulga shrugged. "At home everything is underwater," he said flatly. "My grandmother and my sisters are sitting on the bed. Pedro, too, unless Tío Pepe has come for him. You never can tell. Pedro and I always sleep on the floor, but with this rain and all. . . ."

Gilimon looked at the drenched boy standing in front of him. "Come on," he said, "we can't stay here," and led Pulga into the coffee shop.

"Hungry?" Gilimon asked. He did not wait for an answer and ordered a bowl of soup. When it arrived, along with potatoes and yucca, he said, "Where do you live?"

"Over there, up the hill," answered Pulga between spoonfuls.

"With your grandmother?"

Pulga nodded and went on eating.

"What about your parents? No parents?"

Pulga shook his head.

"What's your name?"

"Pulga."

"What do you do for food?"

No answer.

"Just hanging around in the streets all day long?"

"I watch cars in the marketplace. But today a man was there in a black coat. He chased me away."

"So you are out of work now," Gilimon observed with a smile.

Pulga nodded. His bowl was empty. With a sigh he put down the spoon.

"Want another?"

Pulga nodded.

Gilimon motioned to the waiter, then said slowly, "Well, I need a boy for my truck. I had a helper, but he left me in the lurch, just when I must be off again. But I guess you're too young. . . ."

"I'm fifteen," Pulga said quickly.

Gilimon looked at the boy. He couldn't expect to get much out of such a skinny, undersized beanstalk. No strength in those matchstick arms. But then, it was a toss-up. He thought of the helper on his last trip. The fellow was strong as an ox, and bright too, but as lazy as they come. It was no credit to him that the entire load had not been stolen from the truck while he was sitting in the cab, taking it easy. And when he, Gilimon, had told him what he thought of him, the young gentleman took offense and quit.

Pulga was gulping down his second bowl of soup.

Gilimon said, "I'll take you along."

"What!" Pulga's spoon stopped halfway to his mouth.

"You can come along on the truck tomorrow," Gilimon said. "You'll have to tell your people that I don't know for certain when I'm going to be back. Before Christmas, I hope. It depends on the kind of hauling jobs they give me. Whatever it is, that's it. Tomorrow I'll drive over to Cúcuta."

He got up. In his shiny leather jacket he towered above Pulga. "Want to come along?" he asked.

Pulga just nodded.

"Then I'll see you in the morning. My truck will be standing two blocks down the street at the gas station on the corner. Don't forget to tell your people that I don't know when I'll be back. And make sure you're on time. I have to leave at half past three."

Pulga was so flabbergasted that he did not notice that his soup bowl, with a whole potato still in it, had been taken away. In a daze he went outside. Gilimon's huge truck was rolling down the street, disappearing around the corner.

Pulga ran all the way to the gas station, but Gilimon was gone. The truck, however, was there in all its glory.

Deciding to be on the safe side, he did not bother to go home at all. Quick as a cat he climbed up on the truck and hid under the heavy canvas. Tomorrow morning at half past three he was going to be there. On the dot! Except for Pedro, no one in the big house would miss him.

4

MAMÁ MARUJA'S PLACE
Bogotá to Cúcuta

The rain came pouring down again as they drove out of the city.

Pulga sat bolt upright in the cab, staring through the large windshield. Never before had he been inside an automobile. Never before had he seen the city in this way. Dark rows of houses were gliding past him. The Avenida Caracas came zooming into the headlights. A man was walking across the road. A car came whizzing past them. A night watchman was standing in a doorway.

The rain kept beating against the windshield, but

inside the cab it was dry. The windshield wipers swept across the line of sight, left-right, right-left. ... Gradually the lights from the housing developments that stretched far out into the savanna dropped back into nothingness. They had left the city behind.

The countryside was dark, the air gray. The high ragged mountains, the eastern chains of the Andes, merged with the lead-colored masses of clouds. The big truck rolled along the road; the motor hummed monotonously. Gilimon kept looking straight ahead, his hairy fists clenched over the steering wheel.

Pulga stealthily peered up at him.

"How are you doing?" asked Gilimon without taking his eyes off the road.

"Fine," Pulga whispered, still so taken aback by everything that he could hardly speak. His fingers fidgeted along the edges of the suitcase standing between his legs. It was Gilimon's suitcase.

Slowly, very slowly, the darkness in the valleys receded. The green hilltops were the first to be hit by the rays of the rising sun. Eucalyptus trees and weeping willows along the shoulders of the road began to take shape in the morning mist. The savanna spread out before them. The mountains stood out sharply against the lighted sky.

They drove through small villages. People appeared on the road. They came out of the hills, from remote settlements, from scattered hovels in the valleys to take their produce to the town market. A bagful of potatoes or yucca, a basket of Indian corn, a string of onions. The men rode on sturdy little horses; the baskets and bags were carried by mules and women.

Outside of Tunja they stopped for a quick bowl of soup with chunks of meat, potatoes, and onions, and a cup of hot chocolate.

As they were getting ready to drive on, a big green truck turned off the road and stopped in the parking area outside the eating place. A heavy, muscular man leaned out the side window. "Gilimo-o-on," he called. "Gilimo-o-on, what a miracle to run into you! How are things?"

"*Olé*, Polidorio," Gilimon greeted him heartily. "How are things? What do you say? Anything new?"

"Where are you heading?"

"Cúcuta. And you?"

"Bucaramanga. See you again, God willing."

"Right. Have a good trip now!"

"Same to you."

"Good luck!"

In a cloud of stinking black smoke the truck started up and got back onto the road.

"That was Polidorio," said Gilimon happily. "He's been on the road for years, always for the same shipping outfit, the Phoenix." The thought of his friend made him smile. "A great driver," he added, "a great guy."

Pulga nodded absently. He sat straight up in the cab and looked out into this new world, a new green world, which he had not known existed. "What is that place again we're going to?" he asked.

"Cúcuta, didn't I tell you?"

"Oh, yes," Pulga said quickly. After a while he cautiously ventured another question. "Is it far?"

"Yes and no. It all depends on what you mean by far," said Gilimon casually. "It's over by the Venezuelan border."

Pulga had nothing more to ask. The word Cúcuta meant nothing to him and the word Venezuelan even less. But what did it matter? Here he was, sitting in this marvelous giant of a truck, far away from that filthy wet hole in the big dark house in midtown. For the first time in his life he was not hungry. And he had a job! Who would have thought of such a thing? Pulga sat up still straighter. He breathed deeply and raised his head higher. For a moment he thought of Pedro. What was Pedro doing now?

But then his eyes caught sight again of the sunny countryside that kept speeding by as he looked out the windows. His attention was absorbed by a thousand new and strange things: the cows in the pastures, the waving treetops, the play of light and

Mamá Maruja's Place

shadow on the slopes of the mountains. He was not thinking of Pedro anymore.

Gilimon slowed down and turned into a small country road. They followed its winding course through the hills and came to a little sun-bathed valley surrounded by silvery eucalyptus trees. A little brook wound through the green pasture land. Higher up were dark fir trees, and from the rocks fell a stream of water. The hum of the little waterfall filled the peaceful valley. Gilimon stopped outside a barbed-wire fence. On the other side a narrow path led along a field of Indian corn to a small house.

"Is this it?" asked Pulga.

"It? What do you mean? Oh, you think we're in Cúcuta. Think again, if you can. Cúcuta is still a long way off. This is where Mamá Maruja lives. Mamá Maruja is my godmother. I always drop in here whenever I happen to be in the neighborhood. Step on it, Pulga, open the gate. I didn't bring you along just for the ride."

Pulga jumped out as fast as he could and ran up to the fence. Gilimon watched him desperately trying to get the better of the rickety gate that seemed to be resisting him. Finally it was open. Gilimon wondered once again whether he had done the right thing in taking on such a skinny shrimp for his trip. That flea, he feared, was going to be more trouble than he was worth. With a sigh he drove through the gate, up the bumpy dirt road leading to Mamá Maruja's house. Pulga came running behind the truck. A couple of angry barking dogs dashed out from behind the house, and Pulga clambered up the truck like a scared cat. At that moment a woman in a black dress came out of the house. She was thin and angular, with a parched, wrinkled face and strong muscular arms.

When she saw Gilimon, her face lit up. Her dark piercing eyes sparkled, and the network of wrinkles in her taut face relaxed.

"Blessed be the day!" she called out. "This gladdens my heart."

She put her arms around Gilimon and patted his back over and over. "What's new? What do you have to say for yourself?" she asked.

Then her eyes fell on Pulga. "For the love of God," she exclaimed with surprise. "What have you got there?" She tucked a strand of shining black hair back under her man's hat and looked searchingly at Pulga.

"That is my new helper," said Gilimon and laughed. "He is afraid he might be eaten alive."

Mamá Maruja chased the dogs away. "Now you can come down," she said to Pulga.

"Did you bring my suitcase?" asked Gilimon. "Remember it at all times. You must never leave it behind in the cab. I have my money and all my clothes in it."

"And his shaving mirror with the picture of his girl friend stuck to the back," added Mamá Maruja. "And never the same one twice." She shook her head. "I just wonder when you'll get serious, Gilimon. It's time for you to settle down."

Still shaking her head, she led the way to the other side of the house. Gilimon sat down on the wooden bench that was there and stretched out his legs, evidently feeling quite at home. Mamá Maruja picked up the altar cloth that she had been mending and sat down next to him. Chickens were scratching in the dust, pigs and the two dogs were lying outside the door to the smoke-blackened kitchen, and a bleating goat was tugging at its tether. Pulga felt rather strange with all these animals around and kept looking uncertainly at the dogs.

Meanwhile, Mamá Maruja had gotten up again and disappeared into the small kitchen. A moment later she came back with a large bowl of black coffee for Gilimon. She turned to Pulga. "Here, this is for you," she said, and handed him a gourd shell filled with goat's milk. She watched him as he drank greedily.

"Poor child," she said pityingly. "Skin and bones. How did you get hold of him?"

"It just worked out that way," answered Gilimon. "My helper ran away yesterday. Then I found him. I don't expect to get much out of him, but I suppose he's better than no helper at all."

Mamá Maruja turned to Pulga. "What is your name?" she asked.

"Pulga."

"What did you say?"

"Pulga."

"Pulga? Flea? That cannot be your real name, can it?"

Pulga did not answer. Embarrassed, he dug his bare feet into the dust.

"Tell me now, what is your name, your real name?"

Pulga remained silent. He could not understand why Mamá Maruja should want to know his name. No one ever had asked him that question. He almost had forgotten his name himself. Finally he mumbled in a low voice, "Francisco José."

"Francisco José," Mamá Maruja repeated. "That is what I call a nice name. Not like Pulga. Pulga is not right. From now on I will call you Francisco José."

Then she turned again to Gilimon. "And now," she said, "let's hear the news. Are you coming down from Cúcuta?"

"No, I'm on my way there."

"So you still have quite a trip ahead of you."

"That's for certain. We started out this morning at half past three."

"I see," said Mamá Maruja. "I'm going to make soup for you. After that you will feel fit again." She went back into her kitchen.

"But I can't stay long," objected Gilimon. "I want to get past the stretch where García Rovira is before dark."

Mamá Maruja looked out the kitchen door and nodded. "The Rovira crowd are bad," she said. "Robbers, that's what they are. They fight each other and kill at the drop of a hat. When it isn't politics, it's personal. That's the way it is. Francisco José, go and find me some kindling wood, and then carry in some more water, and go and pick a few ears of corn, but nice ones, young and juicy, you hear? I must make some soup for you, Gilimon. You like my *mazamorra*, don't you? After all, the boy has got to eat something."

Gilimon stopped objecting. No one could argue with Mamá Maruja. She would agree with everything, and then proceed as she wanted to in the first place.

Pulga was busy gathering wood and carrying water and picking corn.

Mamá Maruja looked pleased. "That's the kind of boy I ought to have," she said. "I'm not getting younger, Gilimon. . . . There are the sheep that must be watched, the pigs and the goat to be taken care of. Water must be brought in from the brook each day. Firewood must be gathered. The corn must be harvested. And before you know it, it's time again to plant potatoes. . . ." She sighed. "A boy like you would come in handy," she repeated, as Pulga passed by with an armful of kindling.

She disappeared again into her little smoke-blackened kitchen. Gilimon folded his hands over his stomach and closed his eyes.

Pulga looked uncertainly toward the dogs, and then walked off in the direction of the brook, where he had gone to get water. Along the edge of it, on huge boulders, Mamá Maruja's wash was spread out to bleach. Sunlight flickered over the running water and cast delicate designs of bright and dark spots on the ground under the trees. From behind the eucalyptus trees came the steady hum of the waterfall. Pulga walked a short distance and then he jumped to a large, flat boulder halfway across the brook. The clear icy water washed his dirty feet and thin ankles. The sun was burning on his back, the air was warm and soft. Slowly Pulga waded upstream. The water felt like a soothing balm. Near the rocks, where the foaming waterfall came down, Pulga stopped and looked at the spray of droplets that glistened and glittered in a thousand colors under the sunlight.

On a sudden impulse, he took off his stinking rags and flung them on the ground along the edge of the brook. Stark-naked he walked to the waterfall and stood under it. He let the water splash down on him, over his shoulders and his back. He stretched out his arms. Then he bent down, scooped up a handful of fine sand from under the pebbles and began to scour his body. The water streamed down over him. His skin prickled, and his blood began to tingle. He was alive, and his name was Francisco José!

Finally he stepped out from under the falling water and carefully looked over his arms, his legs, his body. He was almost clean. When he saw his dirty clothes, he hesitated for a moment. Then, crouching on his haunches, he began as best he could to scrub his shirt and his pants. He spread them out to dry on the stones, just the way Mamá Maruja's wash was spread out.

With his arms wrapped around his knees, he sat for a while staring at the flecks of foam that drifted past him on the water. They looked like little white flowers, airily dancing along with the whirling currents. He did not know how long he had been sitting there when suddenly he realized that he was being called.

"Francisco José! Francisco José!"

Hastily he slipped on his damp clothes and ran back.

Gilimon already had sat down to eat, and a bowl of steaming soup stood ready for Pulga. He looked sideways at Mamá Maruja, feeling uncertain, almost distrustful. She had called him to come and eat. He could hardly believe it. Hastily he gulped down the big bowl of soup. With a sigh of satisfaction, he put the spoon down and looked gratefully at Mamá Maruja.

When they drove off, she stood at the gate. A woman with a hard and inscrutable face, her strong arms folded over her chest, her back straight. A woman like many others in the mountain country of Colombia, unswerving, God-fearing, and unbendable.

"*Que la* Santa Virgen *les acompañe*," she called out after them. "May the Virgin Mary be with you."

5

TO THE PÁRAMO DEL ALMORZADERO

The road climbed for a long time, then began to slope down again. They drove into the valley of the Chicamocha River. The mountains stretched out endlessly, bare, hard, deserted. Pastel-colored peaks dissolved in the hazy distance. Far below them flowed the Chicamocha River, its banks green, its bed eroded. High and unreachable rose the steep and somber mountain slopes. The highest peaks were hidden in the clouds.

The farther they went the warmer it became. Rattling buses, with misfiring engines and machine-gunning exhausts, their drivers leaning on their horns, dashed past them. Hot dust blew into the cab. The road gravel was picked up by the tires and hurled down over the edge into the valley below.

Sugarcane and tobacco grew on the hillsides, white cattle stood dully at the riverbanks. In the valleys it was burning hot. The trees and bushes were gray with dust; no breeze stirred the date palms. They drove across the bridge over the Chicamocha River and through Capitanejo, the small village on the other side.

Then the road began to climb again. The motor strained, working hard. Once more they were driving into the mountains. The sun lost its force. The light grew dimmer and shadows settled down between the hills. Though it was dark around the trees and bushes, the air was a blaze of red and yellow and orange, a fierce air that did not give off light but instead drained all color from the earth.

Gilimon looked at his watch. "We should not have stayed at Mamá Maruja's as long as we did," he said.

"I thought it was nice," said Pulga from the depths of his heart.

Gilimon looked at him sideways. "You did, did you?" he said. Then, with a teasing little laugh, he added, "What were you up to there? You lost half your tan."

Pulga stared out the window. "I went to the waterfall. I washed up," he mumbled. "All the way under the water. I stood right under it. It was nice."

"Cold, I guess?" said Gilimon.

"Well, no . . . yes, it was cold. But it wasn't bad. The sun was nice and warm. . . ."

"We should not have stayed as long as we did," Gilimon said again. "I don't drive along this stretch in the dark. Too many holdups. The people around here are no good. They work hard, but you can't trust them, and they don't give a damn. They'll shoot you down for no reason, like a bird in the field. And don't imagine that the police will ever do anything about it. They just shrug and raise their arms over their heads."

Gilimon shifted gears. Slowly the truck pulled up the steep and lonely road. "And among themselves," he went on, "they're no better. They think they can settle their accounts by themselves, without the help of the police. An eye for an eye, a tooth for a tooth, that's their way. A nice bunch!"

It was getting unpleasantly cold. Now the mountains were bare of trees. Only frailejóns with long woolly leaves, like donkeys' ears, grew on the slopes between barren dark underbrush. Fog rolled over the mountaintops, settled in the valleys, rose up between the high bushes, and swept in patches over the road.

PULGA

The headlights picked up eerie formations, sweeping ahead of the moving truck. Figures of women in white gauze, luring them on along the narrow road, higher into the darkness, into the cold, into nothingness. . . .

"Damn it all, there we have it!" Gilimon slammed on the brakes so hard that Pulga banged his head into the windshield. With a jolt, the truck came to a stop. The road was blocked with heavy boulders.

From behind the frailejóns along the roadside three men appeared out of the fog. Handkerchiefs covered their faces, and only their eyes were visible under the rims of their sweat-soaked felt hats. In one leap they were at the door of the cab.

"Get out and keep quiet," said the leader without raising his voice.

Gilimon turned to Pulga, but the seat was empty. The door on the other side stood open. Pulga was gone.

Gilimon slowly stepped down, trying to keep his back covered by the truck. The three men surrounded him.

"Where is your helper?"

"Who?"

"Don't try to be funny. Where is your helper, your assistant, whatever you call him? You're not alone."

"The door on this side is open, Chief," called out

one of the highwaymen who had walked around the truck. "Didn't I tell you? He's gone."

"*Caramba*, don't stand there watching the moon!" the chief shouted. "Go and look for him! And be quick about it. I'll watch this one." Then, turning to Gilimon, he said, "Take one false step, and I'll let you have it full in the face! Where's your money?" Expertly he began to search Gilimon.

The two others ran around the truck, looked under it, inside it, among the frailejóns, in the ditch along the shoulder of the road, in the shadows of fallen rocks.

"Got him?" asked the leader impatiently.

"He isn't anywhere," answered the men.

"You're useless! He must be around. He couldn't have gone far. Be sure you get him. I don't want him sneaking up on us from behind. . . ."

From the mountains came a rumbling noise, loud blasts, and the honking of a horn. Yellow spots of light appeared, were gone again, then reappeared around one of the bends in the road.

The leader cursed and swore. "See that? Someone coming along from the Páramo," he said furiously. "Take that stuff off the truck and be quick about it. This fellow has no money on him. Find his bag in the cab. Hurry, there isn't much time left. . . ."

In the rear of the truck the canvas was ripped open, crates and baskets were pulled out and dropped on the ground. Gilimon was knocked out by a blow on his chin. By the time the bus from Cúcuta reached the barricade, the bandits had disappeared.

Now the deserted mountain road suddenly came to life. Passengers carrying bundles, boxes, bags, baskets came tumbling out of the bus. Women dragged children and carried chickens. One man had a live pig under his arm; another clutched an *aguardiente* bottle.

"What happened?"

"The road is blocked."

"A raid, a highway job! They knocked out the driver!"

"A raid! Ave María Purísima!"

They poured some *aguardiente* into Gilimon and helped him to his feet. They offered him another mouthful of *aguardiente* and drowned him in a flood of questions.

Meanwhile, a few of the men had begun to clear the road. The bus driver walked slowly around the truck and surveyed the damage. "They've taken some of your load, and your canvas is torn," he reported to Gilimon.

"How did it happen?" asked someone.

"How many were there?"

Suddenly Gilimon saw Pulga standing in the middle of the crowd. "Where did you come from?" he asked.

"I . . . I just sat there," answered Pulga, his voice slightly hoarse.

"Where? Where were you sitting?"

"There . . . under the truck."

"Under the truck? Impossible! They looked under the truck!"

"I did sit there. . . ."

Gilimon looked at him in disbelief. Then he caught sight of something Pulga held clutched against his body. "What have you got there? Is that my suitcase?" he asked unnecessarily.

Pulga nodded.

"You have to report this robbery in Pamplona," advised the bus driver. "Otherwise they may think that you made away with the stuff yourself. Those fellows are gone for good. They'll never get caught."

Gilimon nodded vaguely. "Yes, yes . . ." he said, still unable to think clearly. "I'm going to report it right away. Right away . . . in Pamplona."

"A lucky thing for you that we happened to come along," the bus driver said. "Otherwise they might have gotten away with the whole load. They might have done away with you, too—kkrrsh." To make quite clear what he meant he moved his hand swiftly across his throat. "We should have been past here long before this. I don't like to be on this part of the road after dark, but we had trouble up on the Páramo. Well, I don't have to tell you anything, I guess."

The passengers, with their assorted treasures, climbed back into the bus. The children, the chickens, the pig, the cardboard boxes, the filled baskets, and the bulky bags were stowed away, for better or worse, in the aisle. The driver sat down behind the wheel; his helper jumped up on the running board.

"Good-bye now."

"Good-bye and many thanks."

"Not at all."

"Good luck...."

The bus started moving. Honking its horn it rolled downhill.

Gilimon and Pulga drove on into the mountains, up and up to the Páramo del Almorzadero. It was dark and bitter cold, and the wind was pitiless. Pulga sat huddled up in the corner of the cab.

"Seriously now, tell me where you were hiding," said Gilimon.

"Under the truck."

"Those fellows looked everywhere," Gilimon said slowly. "All along the road and up behind the frailejóns. They looked under the truck, too...."

"I was sitting up on the axle."

"On the what?"

"On the axle between the wheels."

"With my suitcase?"

"Yes."

"On the axle between the wheels with a suitcase." Gilimon was completely dumbfounded. "First I have to pull him out from under my truck where he's asleep between the wheels, and then he climbs up on the axle. What do you suppose would have happened if the truck had moved, you ass! Don't you understand that you would have been crushed to a pulp? What were you thinking of? Tell me!"

"I was not thinking at all," admitted Pulga sheepishly. "I was afraid . . . and . . . and you told me that I must look out for the suitcase. You said that I should never leave it behind in the truck."

Gilimon said nothing further. He looked once or twice out of the corner of his eye at the benumbed little boy sitting there next to him. His helper. After a while he mumbled more to himself than to Pulga, "We can thank our stars that the bus from Cúcuta came along. Otherwise not much would be left, that's for certain. The way it was, we got away by the skin of our teeth. In Pamplona I'll have to report the whole thing to the police."

"I thought you said that the police would do nothing," said Pulga. He was not very eager to have anything to do with the police. Policemen had never been particularly friendly to him, and his love for them was lukewarm at best.

"What I said was that they would never find out who held us up. But I have to report such things the first chance I get. In this case, that means Pamplona. Just to keep things straight, you know. Otherwise I have to pay for the damage out of my own pocket. What's the matter? Are you cold?"

Pulga nodded, his teeth chattering.

"There's an old *ruana* under the seat. Take it—you can have it."

The truck hummed along across the bare deserted tableland, over the roof of the world, across the Páramo del Almorzadero. The headlights swept over the hard frozen ground. No trees, no bushes, nothing seemed to be growing.

Once in a while the dark cold expanse of a landlocked lake appeared. Sometimes the yellow light caught huge, eerie boulders ground smooth by driving winds, faded and shaped by endless rains. Like mighty monsters turned into stone, they rose up from the darkness and fell back again into their world of shadows.

The wind howled around the truck. Cold and smooth as metal, the sky hung suspended over the black countryside. There was no trace of life anywhere, no hut, no animal, no light. Dark and lonely and ice-cold. Pulga sat huddled up in his *ruana*. His head dropped down on his chest.

So they drove on to Pamplona.

6

THE ENCOUNTER AT THE COFFEE SHOP

"I was afraid so," said Gilimon. "We're too late. Everything is closed."

The stopover at Pamplona had taken a great deal of time. They had arrived in the middle of the night, slept for a few hours, and then gone to the police station early in the morning.

But the man whose job it was to receive the report could not be found anywhere. They finally got hold of him hours later, and when everything had been straightened out, more time had been lost.

Late that morning they had driven on to Cúcuta.

The sun was high, and the farther they drove the hotter it became, a withering, tropical heat. Pulga kept his newly acquired *ruana* on until he almost melted.

They arrived in Cúcuta at midday. The warehouse where they were to deliver their freight and the freight offices were closed. The little border town lay panting in the noonday heat. A few cars with Venezuelan license plates drove along the streets. Here and there a shopkeeper stood in the door of his shop. But most people sat at home, in their dark houses with closed shutters, in the draft provided by open doors. The bare hills surrounding the town were scorched. A few goats and donkeys walked about the barren land, between high cactuses and thorny shrubs.

"Come along, we might as well get something to eat first," said Gilimon.

In the little coffee shop, where a big fan kept the hot air astir, blaring music made a hellish racket. They sat down in a corner from which they could keep an eye on the truck. Pulga held the suitcase tightly between his knees.

A thin, swarthy man in a snow-white shirt, yellow shoes, and a brand-new Panama hat walked slowly past the coffee shop. A moment later he appeared again, this time from the opposite direction. He came back a third time, then stepped inside and walked straight up to the table where the two were seated.

"Gilimon Naranjo!" he called out. "It's been a long, long time!"

For a moment Gilimon looked at the newcomer in utter surprise. "So help me, Fermin, I didn't recognize you! All dressed up like that. How are things? All right, it seems!"

"Could not be better," said Fermin.

He sat down, lighted a cigarette, and ordered a round of beer. Leaning back, he rolled his cigarette between his nimble brown fingers, examining Gilimon, who looked tired and showed that he had not had a good sleep in a long while.

Fermin was the picture of a man who was pleased with himself. His movements were smooth and meant to give the impression that he was a man of the world. He flicked his cigarette away and began to poke around between his teeth with a toothpick. He had three gold teeth in front. On his right arm was the tattoo of a snake that wound around and around, its head with forked tongue extending to the upper arm. When Fermin let his muscles play, the snake seemed to be alive. Pulga could hardly stop looking at it.

Finally the beer arrived, and the two men talked awhile about the weather and whatever else happened to come to their minds.

Then Fermin said, "Is that your truck standing out there?"

Gilimon nodded. "I still have to get it unloaded." He explained what had happened.

Fermin tapped the toothpick against his teeth and nodded. "Oh, yes," he said understandingly. "One never runs out of problems."

"You can say that again," Gilimon agreed.

"I suppose you have your next load all lined up?"

"Not yet," Gilimon said. "But coffee for Barranquilla is always easy to get, I suppose."

Fermin raised his eyebrows and grinned. "I'm glad it's you and not me riding that long stretch to Barranquilla. The road is bad, and hot as blazes."

"Can't be helped. It's my line of work," said Gilimon resignedly. "Fortunately my truck is in good shape. It gives me little trouble."

Fermin nodded. "Yes, I can see that. It's a good truck," he added approvingly and ordered another round.

"I might have a load for you," he said casually. "I have a couple of things to ship and I'm looking for a good, reliable truck. If you can help me out. . . . After all, we're old friends, aren't we? There's good money in it for you. The whole thing doesn't amount to much. You turn around, and you've earned your share."

Gilimon didn't answer immediately, but kept looking at Fermin. "What sort of freight is it?" he asked dubiously. "Not stolen goods by any chance?"

"Stolen?" Fermin asked indignantly. "Who do you think I am?" He turned up the palms of his hands. "My hands are clean," he said solemnly. "It's just that I happen to need a truck and that I saw you sitting here when I passed by. But if you're not interested...."

"Where do you want the stuff taken?" Gilimon asked.

Fermin ordered more beer. "Oh, it would take too long to explain now," he said vaguely. "I better leave that to the boss."

"The boss?" Gilimon asked. "You have a boss? I thought the job was for you—"

"I handle this thing together with a few other fellows," Fermin interrupted. "And, of course, a well-run business needs a boss, don't you think? If you come along I'll explain the whole thing to you. I'm living now in a house on the Río Seco. We can talk there in a leisurely way. But one thing I can tell you right now. If you accept, you won't regret it. You get well paid for what you have to do. Just look at me...." He passed his flat, brown hand over his brand-new shirt and proudly pointed to his gold watch.

Fermin got up. "Think about it this afternoon," he said. "I still have a few things to take care of. I'll be back here around seven o'clock."

Aimlessly he let his eyes wander outside. A woman with a bundle of washed clothes on her head walked past. A donkey burdened with a load of sugarcane was driven along by a little barefoot boy. A man, sweat pouring down his face, was trying desperately to get his ancient pickup truck going.

Fermin pursed his lips, then smiled condescendingly, full of self-assurance. His gold teeth were shining. "All that drudgery. It makes me sick just to watch it, when money lies around in the street. All you have to do is bend down and pick it up."

With these profound remarks he vanished.

7

THE HOUSE ON THE RÍO SECO

Three men were sitting at a shaky table on the porch of the house on the Río Seco, playing dominoes by the light of a kerosene lamp. Their surly faces looked eerie in the dim light.

One of the men put down a domino. "A three or a one," he said. "Your turn, Adonias." The speaker, Angelito, was small and thin with a pointed rat's head and nervous, unsteady eyes. Adonias carefully placed his domino, moving his thick, hairy fingers with remarkable precision.

The third man, Octavio, poured down the rest of

his beer and shoved the empty bottle across the table. "It's taking a long time," he said.

"Yes, a long time," Angelito agreed. His eyes moved unsteadily. The game continued.

"Was that the last of the beer?"

A slovenly young woman, sitting at the far end of the porch, disappeared hastily into one of the large rooms of the dark house and came back with a couple of bottles of beer. On the bare, hard ground in front of the porch children were playing among the dogs and pigs lying about. A goat marched across the porch. When the young woman chased it away impatiently, the goat became frightened and jumped down the wooden steps, barely skirting an old woman who sat huddled up on them. She was very old and thin, with a wrinkled face and long disheveled hair. In the folds of her grimy skirt she held a child. Her bony fingers, with long black nails, were searching through the child's greasy, curly hair.

Suddenly the dogs became excited; they pointed their ears, growled, and jumped up. Octavio raised his head. "Someone is coming," he said. "I suppose it's Fermin."

"I suppose so," said Angelito. "I wonder whether he found someone."

"It's got to be someone reliable. . . ."

"Yes, that's for sure."

The House on the Río Seco

By now the humming noise of the heavy truck could be heard clearly, and the dogs took off, barking wildly.

A moment later the big truck came swaying across the plot of land outside the house and stopped. Fermin, Gilimon and Pulga stepped out. Gilimon looked around. His eyes took in the low wooden house tucked away in the hills overgrown with cactuses and agaves. The rigid pointed leaves of the agaves thrust like spears into the starry tropical sky, where a sickle moon was floating on its back between the hills. In the dim light the empty wooden house looked decrepit.

Gilimon raised his eyebrows. "Is this the place?" he asked.

"This is it," answered Fermin. "Come along."

He walked up the steps to the porch. "Don Ramon?" he asked the men.

Angelito motioned with his rat's head to a row of dark rooms that opened on the wooden porch. "He's there. He's waiting."

Pulga looked in the direction Angelito had indicated.

In the open door of one of the rooms a man with a broad back and heavy shoulders was sitting, leaning back in his chair against the doorframe. A yellow straw hat, pulled down to his eyebrows, covered most of his face.

Fermin motioned to Gilimon to go with him, and the men at the table pushed their chairs away and followed. They stood around Don Ramon in a circle, speaking in low voices. Pulga could not hear what was being said. Fermin was picking his three golden teeth with a matchstick. Angelito kept looking around, his eyes moving restlessly. After a while the three domino players disappeared inside the house while Gilimon, with Fermin close behind, went off to park the truck in the rear. Only Don Ramon remained in the same spot, the straw hat still pulled down over his face.

Pulga stood undecided in the yard outside among the group of gaping children, not knowing what to do. He would have liked best to run after Gilimon when he returned with Fermin. But Gilimon had walked straight past him into the house, without saying a word or even looking at him.

One of the dogs came growling toward Pulga, his upper lip curled. A boy, who looked about thirteen, gave him a kick, and the yelping animal vanished between the slats under the porch.

"What's your name?" the boy asked.

"Pulga."

"Oh."

"What's your name?"

"Camilo."

"Oh."

"They're going tonight, hey?" said the boy in a low voice.

"Yes, I think so," answered Pulga vaguely. Just what Fermin wanted them to do was not clear to him, but he felt somehow that it was not completely aboveboard. He studied the other boy more closely. Evidently Camilo knew more than he did. He must get him to talk and find out what was going on.

"Are you . . . do you go along, too?" he asked.

Camilo shrugged. "Maybe yes, maybe no. That depends. . . ."

"Yes," said Pulga, trying to sound knowledgeable. "Yes, that's for Don Ramon to decide. After all, he's the boss."

Camilo looked instinctively in the direction of Don Ramon. The man in the doorway had taken off his straw hat. He passed his short stubby fingers a few times over his face and through his long, wavy light-gray hair. Then his hand moved searchingly over his chest and came back with a cigarette. Patiently he struck a match on the sole of his shoe and held it up to his cigarette. For one moment the bright flicker of flame in the darkness lit up his face.

It was a remarkable face, broad and strong, with high cheekbones and deep furrows. The dark, tanned skin contrasted sharply with the silvery hair. The mouth was fleshy and cruel. But the most striking feature was his eyes. They were a clear, light, transparent green, the color of sea water. Cold and sharp, with no warmth in them.

"Yes, Don Ramon will decide, and then, too. . . ." Camilo did not finish what he was about to say, and Pulga had to bite his tongue to hide his impatience. To ask too many questions was risky.

"Oh, well," he said casually. "We'll soon find out, once they get it all straightened out."

"That's it," Camilo agreed. He again looked up to where Don Ramon was sitting and whispered to Pulga, "He doesn't feel quite right tonight. Don Ramon is nervous. Otherwise he would not smoke."

"But . . . I guess he does know the ropes," Pulga whispered back. "It's not the first time. . . ."

"Of course not, but last time things didn't work out. The trucks were shot at. One is standing up there in the hills, a complete loss." Camilo stroked his face just as Don Ramon had done. "Nothing like that ever happened to us before. Things always went smoothly. Don Ramon thinks someone has betrayed him. He thinks. . . ."

"Well?" Pulga asked.

"He thinks that it's one of our own men, but he doesn't know who. When he finds out. . . ."

Pulga nodded understandingly. "Whoever it is had better start writing his last will."

"Right," Camilo agreed. "And he's going to find

out. This morning I heard him talk things over with Obdulia." Camilo moved his head almost unnoticeably in the direction of the old woman in the black dress, who was still sitting on the bottom step of the stairs. The young woman had taken away the child to feed it.

"So, what did they say?"

"Don Ramon said that she should turn his cup over. The cup from which he drank his chocolate this morning."

"Oh, and . . . did she do it?"

Camilo nodded. "She put it on the shelf in the kitchen. I saw it there myself."

"And what," Pulga began, but Camilo dug his elbow into his ribs.

"Quiet now," Camilo warned. "Here they come. And remember, not a word of what I told you."

"Not a word," Pulga swore, though he had decided long since to tell Gilimon everything as soon as he had a chance. Just imagine, their beautiful truck might be shot to pieces tonight. Pulga could not bear the thought.

The footsteps of the men in the empty, dark house sounded hollow and hard. "We are ready," one of the men said to Don Ramon.

Don Ramon stood up in front of them, legs apart. His short, muscular arms were bent at the elbows and held slightly away from his body. He looked hard at each of his men with those keen, strangely clear eyes.

"Wait for me by the trucks," he said, and remained standing until the men had disappeared. Then he motioned to the old woman at the foot of the stairs. "Come," he said.

Slowly she rose to her feet, climbed up the stairs, shuffled across the porch, and went inside the house with Don Ramon. The door slammed behind them.

Pulga moved to follow Gilimon, but Camilo held him back. "There's no need to hurry," he said in a low voice. "You can be sure they won't leave before Don Ramon gives the order. And before he does that, Obdulia must read the future for him. Come along, I want to know what Obdulia has to say, and I know how to find out." He pulled Pulga along with him through the porch slats, and they crawled on their bellies under the house. It was pitch dark and smelled of garbage.

Over their heads they could hear the wooden planks creak under the heavy footsteps of Don Ramon and the shuffling of the old woman. "You have the cup?" asked Don Ramon, sounding impatient.

"Here . . . here it is, *mijito*," answered the old woman in a soothing tone, as if she were speaking to a child. "Here it is. Be patient now. Everything will be all right. Obdulia is going to read the future for you. Wait now, wait, and be patient." The old voice fell silent. Then for a long while nothing could be heard.

Under the floor Camilo's hand reached out for Pulga's, pulling him farther on. They were lying side by side now. "Over here in the corner is a hole," Camilo whispered. "When you push yourself up, you can see something."

Cautiously they raised themselves and peered through an opening where a few boards were missing. Straight ahead was a crude wooden partition with wide cracks. In the dimly lit room on the other side Don Ramon was sitting on a chair. Obdulia was crouched on the floor in front of him, a lighted candle in one hand, an earthenware cup without a handle in the other. Slowly she turned the cup over in her hand, studying the veinlike lines that had formed in the brown dregs.

"There . . . there," she said soothingly. "There I see it all. The trees, the river, but the trucks do not cross the river . . . no, not across the river . . . not this time . . . not as before." She shook her head thoughtfully, again turned the cup in her bony dirty hand, and stared into it. "Look, there it is again . . . farther down . . . narrow and steep . . . there it goes across. . . ." Suddenly the hand holding the candle moved jerkily, the flame flickered, almost went out, then flickered up again. "And here . . . here is a face . . . yes, it is a face. It is not a good face. . . ."

Pulga saw Don Ramon bend forward. "Yes," he said. "Yes . . . who is it? Can you see? Tell me. . . ."

But the old woman shook her head. "One against three," she said. "One against three. Watch out." Breathing heavily, she got up from the floor and stood in front of Don Ramon. "That is all," she said. "There is nothing more I have to say."

Don Ramon rose slowly from his chair.

"Now we must get out of here as fast as we can," Camilo whispered. Crawling hurriedly on their hands and knees, with Camilo leading the way in the labyrinth of rotten boards, they came out on the side of the house. Before standing up, Camilo looked around carefully, then slipped out with Pulga close behind.

When Don Ramon arrived where the trucks were parked, Camilo and Pulga were already there.

8

THE PROPHECY OF THE OLD WOMAN

The trucks moved along through the hilly countryside, dense with cactuses, thorny bushes, and blooming agaves, whose yellow flowers on yard-long stems rose into the velvet sky. The sickle of the moon had long since gone down behind the hills, and the sky shone with the brilliance of countless stars. There was no road, only a deep carved-out track. Perhaps it was the worn bed of a dried-up river, possibly the Río Seco, or what was left of a long-untraveled road.

"So that is what they needed another truck for,"

said Gilimon. "One of theirs got shot to pieces. A fine mess. Here we are in the middle of it, Pulga!"

Ahead of them they could make out the dark outline of the truck in which Adonias, Camilo, and Don Ramon were riding. Behind them followed the third truck driven by Fermin, with Angelito and Octavio next to him.

Gilimon had stuck to his guns when Fermin wanted to take over his truck. "Out of the question," he had said. "No one is going to take over my truck."

Fermin had been angry. He had lit a cigarette, but Don Ramon made him crush it out. Afterward Fermin had fallen back into his old habit of picking his gold teeth with a purple-colored matchstick.

Don Ramon had said nothing. He just looked at each of his men. Finally, with a movement of his eyes, he ordered Fermin into Octavio's truck. Before taking his seat in the lead truck, he again had scrutinized his men, one after another, with his cold, penetrating eyes. It seemed to Pulga that his glance had dwelled longest on Angelito. But perhaps not. Perhaps Don Ramon had stared longest at Gilimon and his helper.

Hours seemed to have passed since their departure. The trucks, bumping and swaying, were moving through a deep gully. Pulga stared at the starry

The Prophecy of the Old Woman

heavens that slowly moved along over the edge of the rim.

"Do you know where we are going?" he asked, turning to Gilimon.

"They did not tell me, but it's not hard to guess. Of course, across the border."

"Smuggling goods?" Pulga asked rather superfluously.

"You said it," Gilimon agreed with a sarcastic laugh.

"What is on the truck?"

"Coffee, if you ask me. But hold your tongue now for a while, Pulga. I've got to watch out here. . . ."

They were driving now over a narrow path under high trees. The bright starry sky was hidden by the high dark treetops. Branches scraped against the wide body of the truck as they crept along at a very slow pace.

Suddenly Fermin's face appeared at the driver's window. "Pssst . . . stop! We're going the wrong way," he whispered urgently.

Gilimon stared ahead. "There goes the other truck," he answered. "Where it goes, I go."

"Yes, but we're going the wrong way. We've driven past the spot where the trail branches off down the river. I don't understand what those fellows up there are doing. Adonias knows every inch of the way, and so does Don Ramon. I don't get it. . . . Wait here." He ran ahead to catch up with the first truck.

Gilimon stopped. "If they turn back," he whispered to Pulga, "and the truck ahead turns down toward the river, I'm going to drive straight on as fast as I can. Somehow we'll manage to get the cargo off the truck. I don't feel like getting shot to pieces."

"I don't either," said Pulga a little worried.

"But we have to watch out. They're an unpredictable bunch. The old fellow doesn't look anybody's fool."

"Don Ramon has a gun, and I suppose the others are armed, too," Pulga remarked. "Suppose they take a pot shot at our tires."

"They know better than that. They won't dare use their guns around here. We're right next to the border, if you ask me. Come, let's go and listen to what they're saying." He stepped down and walked up to the first truck, where Fermin stood arguing, apparently to no avail. Pulga followed right on his heels.

"We've got to go back," said Fermin emphatically. "We've gone far beyond the trail that leads down to the river. Angelito says so, too."

"Yes, that's right," mumbled Adonias.

"We'll drive on," said Don Ramon.

"But farther up there is no trail," Fermin objected.

The Prophecy of the Old Woman

"We'll make one," answered Don Ramon.

"But Angelito says—" Fermin tried again.

"Enough of that. Let's go!" Don Ramon ordered.

The first truck slowly got moving again. Fermin shook his head. "I don't know what Don Ramon has in mind," he said to Gilimon. "Well, he's not getting any younger. Maybe he's too old to think clearly and be the boss. You know how these things are. They hate to let go. I've been noticing that for quite a while. Well, so far everything has worked out smoothly and—"

"Has it?" Gilimon interrupted. "But last time you lost a truck, didn't you?"

Fermin looked startled. "How do you know? Who told you?"

Pulga watched Gilimon. He looked scared.

"I saw it standing among the cactuses," Gilimon answered. "Didn't you know that I've got two eyes in my head?"

Fermin shrugged. "You must have been mistaken," he said. "We never run into trouble. Our organization is first-rate." He walked back to his truck.

"You can see that fellow did not choke to death on his first lie," Gilimon commented when they were on their way. "Or do you suppose Camilo told you a fairy tale?"

The trail was getting worse by the minute. Finally

there was nothing left of it but a rut along a steep slope. The trucks were leaning dangerously to one side as they bumped along over fallen trees and scraped against heavy boulders. Pebbles rattled sharply against the body of the truck.

"This isn't the best way to make a truck last," mumbled Gilimon. "Why did they pick this road when there's another?"

"The old woman told him," Pulga answered.

"What?"

"The old woman told him. The one sitting on the steps. Her name is Obdulia. She said that we should not take the road along the river, but go on here . . . farther down. She read Don Ramon's future."

"How come you know that?" Gilimon asked. "Is this another thing Camilo told you?"

Pulga shook his head. "I heard it myself. I saw it, too, with Camilo. She read his future from the chocolate cup he used for breakfast."

"Good heavens," said Gilimon scornfully. "And Fermin calls this a top-notch organization. First I am made to think that Fermin works for himself. Then I learn that Don Ramon is the boss. And finally I find out that an old witch has the last word. How did I get into this mess! Well, Pulga, it's a good thing I know now. As soon as I have my money, we'll kiss them all good-bye."

"There was something else Obdulia said. She said, 'One against three,' and that he had to watch out for that. I mean, Don Ramon should watch out for it."

"One against three," Gilimon repeated. "What did she mean by that?"

"I don't know," Pulga answered.

"One against three. . . ." Gilimon stared ahead racking his brain. A confused picture loomed up in his mind. Three . . . three . . . and one. . . . It did not quite jibe. And still, it seemed to belong somehow. . . . What was it? Where had he seen that? This afternoon . . . this evening? He could not remember.

The trees began to thin out. It grew lighter. They were driving downhill now, along a growth of tall, softly shining sugarcane, then on through the lush grass of a pasture bordered with trees and bushes. White cattle moved in the tall grass, lowing eerily. From farther down came the rushing sound of water, and soon they arrived at the river, splashing and whirling its way between the boulders in its shallow bed.

Like monstrous animals, the trucks crept down the embankment and into the river. They bumped over big stones. Water rushed with a hissing sound through the wheels and whirled up in a filmy crest in front of the bumpers. Slowly they reached the other side and moved up onto dry land. Again they drove past fields of sugarcane, along narrow winding trails, until finally they reached a small farm building.

As the trucks pulled up, a group of men came out of the shed on one side of the house. "I did not think you would come tonight," said one of them to Don Ramon. "The trail is being watched. Didn't you run into trouble? They must have been tipped off. They are up there tonight."

Don Ramon motioned with his chin. "We drove along down below, a couple of miles downstream."

Another man nodded approvingly. "Nice work."

The men started to unload the cargo from the trucks into the shed, where it was piled up behind bundles of cornstalks. Don Ramon watched the unloading, an unlit cigarette between his lips. When Fermin came by with a bag on his shoulder, he called out, "You have a match?"

Fermin put down the bag, produced a box of matches from one of his pockets, and proceeded to light a match. For a second Don Ramon looked straight at the bright little flame of the purple-colored matchstick, then lit his cigarette from it and turned away. Fermin lifted the bag onto his shoulder and disappeared into the shed.

When they finished the unloading, Adonias reported to the boss, "We're all done. That's it."

Don Ramon nodded. "Take the last truck," he said. "Fermin will ride with me."

One behind the other, the trucks moved off. The stars grew pale, the flaming red of the rising sun spread across the sky, driving the night away. The grassland on the riverbanks appeared dew-white in the early morning light. In the distance the edge of the forest remained dark. The underbrush and heavy branches of the giant trees clung to the night.

The trucks clambered up the embankment on the far side and followed the tracks they had left behind in the long grass, moving ahead through banks of fog. A few zebus, wading heavily through the white grass, raised their heads, mooed softly, and stared at the passing trucks.

"What's going on now?" said Gilimon. He leaned over the steering wheel and peered through the windshield.

The truck ahead had stopped. Don Ramon and Fermin stepped out. In single file they walked across the grassland. Fermin was in front, his shoulders drooping; Don Ramon, shotgun over his shoulder, followed close behind. The side door of the truck remained open.

The zebus raised their heads and looked after them, startled. Two small figures, up to their hips in the swaying grass, marched toward the edge of the forest.

Gilimon stepped out. With Pulga right on his heels, he walked up to the head truck where Camilo was sitting all by himself in the cab. The three men from the hindmost truck joined them.

No one spoke. Their eyes followed the two dark figures that grew smaller and smaller in the distance. Don Ramon and Fermin almost had reached the edge of the forest. For a few more moments they could be seen in the light of the rising sun. Then they were swallowed up by the dark shadow of the trees.

For a long while nothing happened. The zebus calmed down and were grazing again. The sun rose higher, shedding its brilliant light over the small savanna. A bird trilled throatily. Then, from far away, they heard a single muffled sound.

"Ave María, Virgen Santisima," murmured Angelito. He looked shyly at his comrades.

They all made the sign of the Cross.

Octavio was the first to speak. He turned to Camilo. "What happened, do you know?" he asked hoarsely.

"I . . . I have no idea," stammered Camilo.

"But you were with them."

Camilo nodded.

"Did they quarrel?"

Camilo shook his head.

"But something must have happened."

"No, nothing. Nothing at all. Fermin drove and

The Prophecy of the Old Woman

Don Ramon was sitting next to him. He kept looking at Fermin, but he said nothing, and Fermin did not say anything either. And then, after we crossed the river, when we were driving across the grassland, Fermin began picking his teeth with a matchstick. Don Ramon kept looking at him. All the while he kept looking at Fermin poking around with his matchstick against his three gold teeth. Fermin does that all the time, but Don Ramon kept looking at him as though he was noticing the habit for the first time. And then he said, 'One against three . . . that is it, one against three. . . .' " Camilo paused to take a breath.

"Then he ordered Fermin to stop, and they got out. Fermin did not ask why. He said nothing. He did not resist either. He did just as he was told, as though he was hypnotized. But he was afraid, I could see that. Don Ramon said nothing more. He was not even angry or anything like that. He just took his gun along."

The men looked at one another.

"One against three," Angelito repeated. "Why one against three? What does that mean?" He turned to Camilo. "What did Don Ramon have in mind when he said that?"

Camilo glanced quickly at Pulga. "I wouldn't know," he said.

9

DRIVING DOWN TO THE COAST
Cúcuta to Barranquilla

The truck, heavily laden with bales of coffee, rumbled along the road through the mountains. It was the hottest time of day, the road was bad and dusty, and they made slow headway.

"*Olé*, I'm glad that's over," said Gilimon.

"Me, too," Pulga agreed heartily.

When Don Ramon had returned, Pulga had been scared to death. Alone, gun over his shoulder, his cold cruel eyes had looked at them all, one after another.

"That's that," he had said. "That's what comes of

trying to double-cross me." Without another word they all had climbed into their trucks and driven back to the house on the Río Seco.

Pulga had had no chance to talk again to Camilo, who disappeared into the big empty house together with the other men. That was the last he saw of Camilo. The old woman had been sitting on the steps and gazed after them as they drove away. It seemed that she had been sitting there all night long. Pulga hardly had dared think of the night's adventure, let alone talk about it with Gilimon.

Now he said hesitatingly, "What was it that Fermin did?"

"He informed the Border Police when and where the trucks would go across."

"But I thought he was working together with Don Ramon. I thought they were friends."

"Well, they were for that matter."

"But why then would he want to inform on Don Ramon?"

"Maybe Fermin was fed up with being an underling," Gilimon remarked dryly. "He wanted to be on top. The whole thing almost cost me my truck and you your job. It's even possible that we might not have come out alive."

Pulga thought of the old woman Obdulia. With a sigh he said, "It's a good thing Don Ramon was forewarned."

A smile, almost of admiration, passed over Gilimon's face. "Don Ramon is nobody's fool, believe you me. Nothing escapes him, and he doesn't believe that things happen by accident. When he saw what kind of matches Fermin was using, he drew his own conclusions, and Fermin's fate was sealed. That Don Ramon, I watched him carefully. You can't bargain with a man like that. He's utterly ruthless."

"Was there anything special about those matches?" Pulga asked.

"Yes," Gilimon replied. "They were purple."

Around a bend in the road a man appeared on horseback, leading a large herd of cattle. He waved his arm, and Gilimon slowed down. Pulga stared across the billowing mass of bluish-white animals without really seeing them. He did not understand what Gilimon meant. The old woman had said nothing about matches. She had never even seen Fermin's matches, and yet she. . . .

He looked at the cows whose horns swayed to-and-fro as they pressed on. Slowly, lazily, the herd kept moving past the truck. Their horns scraped along the cab, their heavy bodies pressed against the wheels and the side planks above. A group of cowboys made the last animals close ranks.

The road was free again, and the truck, its motor humming, resumed speed. Passenger cars and buses

Driving Down to the Coast

that also had been held up by the herd dashed past them at high speed. Clouds of yellow dust blew into the hot cab.

"So help me, what a road!" said Gilimon, venting his annoyance. "I won't feel sorry when we get to the coast. At least the road along the ocean is good. No potholes, no dust, and the salty sea wind...."

"Along the ocean...." Pulga repeated vaguely. He was still racking his brain over Gilimon's last remark. What did it mean?

"Yes, a mighty expanse of water without end. That is the ocean."

"Oh," said Pulga, as though he understood. He stared at the cloud of yellow dust hanging over the road. The mountains, the hills, the small plots of farmland slowly passed by.

"I don't understand what the purple matches have to do with it," he said. "Why purple? Matches are white, aren't they?"

"Not in Venezuela," Gilimon answered.

"But the old woman," Pulga persisted stubbornly, "Obdulia...."

Gilimon nodded. "Yes. She knew!"

"But she was sitting on the steps. She did not even look up. How could she know what sort of matches Fermin had on him? And she read Don Ramon's future and told him that he should not take the road along the river, and...."

"Yes," said Gilimon, and in his voice was an undertone of half-acknowledged respect. "Who knows what powers those old women call up with their black magic and their herbs they gather on dark nights? Who knows what they see in the lines of your hand, in the whirl of running water? Who knows what they hear in the wind? Don't underrate them. . . . They know."

Silently they rode on through the yellowish haze. Now and then a car shot past them. They overtook a man on a donkey, a woman with a bundle of kindling wood on her back, children with tin cans of water on their shoulders walking back to their homes in the hills. They stopped for a snack at a road stand, and later had a bottle of lemonade at a gas station where they filled up the tank.

It was late in the afternoon when Gilimon pulled up to the side of the road. Steam poured out from under the hood; the radiator was boiling. "I thought I was smelling something," said Gilimon. "Sure enough, the radiator has sprung a leak. This morning I filled it up at Cúcuta before we left, and I checked it again when we stopped for gas. And now this! Well, there's nothing to do but get water somewhere. Take the can, Pulga, and make it fast."

If Pulga's job had been easy until now, it was no longer. More and more frequently they had to stop to get water down below at the edge of a winding

Driving Down to the Coast

brook, or at some small river in the valley, or up in the hills from a crack in the rocks.

Evening fell. In the drab little villages they passed through, women sat crouched in the dark doorways of their houses, men loitered outside the village inns, children played in the dim light. Gradually the hustle-bustle of daily life subsided.

Finally they left the mountains behind and were driving on the road that led north to Valledupar and Santa Marta and the Caribbean Sea. The big road ran along through the lowlands where the heat of the past day still lingered.

For hours they drove deep into the night. The headlights cut through the darkness over pastures and cotton and sesame fields along both sides of the road. The wall of a small forsaken inn loomed up, plastered with advertising posters for beer and Coca-Cola and a blackboard with the day's menu in faded letters.

Gilimon pulled up outside the inn and turned the ignition key. He stretched out his legs and arms and wearily bent backward, breathing deeply. Except for short stops to eat, buy gas, and fill up the radiator, they had been driving all day. For close to twelve hours they had been traveling through dust and heat, over bad roads, along sloping hills and deep gullies, with the constant humming of the motor in their ears.

The quiet of night settled over the dusty truck. Dark mango trees rustled in the night wind. A little brook somewhere farther along the road murmured steadily. A dog barked, but inside the little house all remained quiet. Gilimon folded his arms over the steering wheel; his head dropped down. He was asleep.

But Pulga could not follow his example. Restlessly fidgeting on his seat, he stared through the windshield into the darkness. Stars glittered in the deep-blue sky; a lisping breeze swayed the tops of the trees and the foliage. Things remembered came to Pulga's mind: the events of the morning, the faces of Don Ramon and Fermin, the phantom of the old woman crouched on the stairs. She had known. . . .

She had looked into the future! The future! Never before in his hopeless existence had he given the future any thought. Now he wondered what tomorrow would bring. How long would this journey with Gilimon last? Where were they going? When would they be back in Bogotá? What would happen to him then? Would Gilimon keep him as his helper? Or was he to fall back into the drab life in the cold grimy house where his grandmother and his sisters were sitting, and where he and Pedro slept on the floor?

What had Pedro thought the day when he had failed to show up? Had he asked about him among their neighbors in the large house or in the street among the boys outside the movie houses? Had he perhaps gone to the square where Pulga had been spending his time as a car watcher? Or had he simply accepted the fact that Pulga had disappeared? Just the way they had accepted the fact that their father no longer came home. They had to take life as it happens. What else can one do?

A person can't swim against the current. If he does, it will only add to his misery. God knows, not much is needed to increase one's burden.

It is best to drift along, like flakes of foam on waters. Drifting flakes of foam? Where had he seen that? Yes, in the little brook in back of Mamá Maruja's cottage. There he had sat in the sun and watched them drift by like white water lilies. A faint smile passed over Pulga's face. That was where he had washed off the grime of the city . . . where he had felt the blood tingle in his veins. And Mamá Maruja! She had called him Francisco José, she had called him to come and sit down to eat! Ave María . . . strange things could happen in this world.

His own grandmother . . . no, he could not recall that his own grandmother had ever. . . . What, in fact, did she. . . . The vague picture of his grandmother was overshadowed by that other face. The tawny face with keen eyes that had looked him over so penetratingly.

Mamá Maruja had nodded to him as though she liked him. "That's the kind of boy I ought to have," he had heard her say to Gilimon. "A boy like you. . . ." She had said it to him, Pulga. A gentle wind blew into the cab over Pulga's disheveled hair. Or was it Mamá Maruja's hand . . . ? He was not sure. Feelings and thoughts became confused, seemed to get lost in the murmur of the brook and the rustling of the wind.

He fell asleep smiling.

10

EDUARDO

The shrill sound of voices and the barking of the dog awakened him. Standing in the early light of dawn in the middle of the drive-in area was a group of unkempt children staring at the truck.

"There's a car here!"

"Ave María, so early?" came a woman's voice from inside the house.

"Yes, a truck, a big one!"

"Who is it?"

"A driver!"

"Eduardo, go and get water," commanded the

voice. "Have the pigs been fed? Is there wood in the kitchen? María, start the fire and tell Clementina to get the batter ready for the *arepas*. . . ."

In the open door of the little inn with a signboard inscribed in crooked letters, *Sufrir es mi Destino*, appeared a sturdy young woman, busily braiding her long jet-black hair. Her reddish, sun-tanned face, her broad build, her strong muscles did not indicate that suffering was her destiny, as the name of her inn dramatically suggested. She had her crew of offspring well in hand, and in a moment they were all put to work, including the smallest, who trotted off to gather kindling wood.

With a quick motion of her head, she flung her tightly braided hair over her shoulder, and with arms folded across her chest, she watched Gilimon and Pulga climb stiffly out of the cab.

"If it isn't Gilimon!" she called out. "How are things? What's new?"

Gilimon was not up to talking so early in the morning. Without giving him a chance to say even a word or two, Benita rattled off all the news:

In Codazzi the cotton pickers had arrived, many of them from as far as Tolima, some with their entire families. Trying to get away from the bandits back home. Ave María, what a situation! And every day things grew worse. Fortunately all was quiet in these parts. There was a lot of traffic along the road; things were moving. Hog flu had broken out in the neighborhood. Yesterday she had slaughtered one of the pigs that did not seem to be getting on as it should. She had been busy till late in the night, which was why she had not heard their truck. Otherwise she always heard everything. A driver from Codazzi had come with the news that her mother was ill. She would have liked to go and see her mother, but how could she? So far away and with all the work to be done here. Every day there was something else, more problems than she cared for.

She turned and called back into the house, "María, is the cocoa ready? Clementina, how are the pancakes coming? Eduardo. . . ."

Gilimon used this interruption to slip away, motioning to Pulga to come along and to bring the suitcase. Though it was still dawn, the heat was oppressive, but under the trees at the brook it was still cool. They scooped up the muddy water from between the stones and splashed it over their skin. Gilimon put on a clean shirt, and Pulga did his best to shake the dust out of his sweat-drenched clothes.

When they came back, the little girls were bustling back and forth with steaming cocoa and golden-yellow *arepas* that had come out of the little round oven next to the house. Over a charcoal fire big chunks of pork were roasting. Gilimon decided to stick to the corn pancakes and cocoa.

To Pulga, who eyed the food greedily, he said, "Let's first see what we can do about the radiator leak. We need cement. Maybe you can find some, Pulga, on the other side of the house. They're building a barn there."

He turned to the boy who had brought in water and was now leaning against the wall, out of sight of his mother. Clearly he was looking for a way out of the chores waiting for him. "What's your name again?"

"Eduardo."

"Can you get me some grease, Eduardo?"

"What?"

"Can you get me some grease?"

"No, we haven't any."

"How about eggs?"

"What?"

"Have you any eggs? Go and get me some eggs from your mother."

With obvious reluctance Eduardo went to carry out what had sounded like an order. Dragging his feet, he disappeared into the house and was back in a moment. Leaning against the door post, he said, "Boiled or fried, my mother wants to know."

"Raw," Gilimon ordered.

When Eduardo finally returned with the eggs, Gilimon cracked the shells open and let the slimy whites run out on the cement that Pulga had found.

He expertly plugged the hole in the radiator with his makeshift mixture.

Pulga had raised his eyebrows at Gilimon's rather careless handling of the precious eggs, but he hadn't dared say a word.

"Here, eat this," Gilimon said, offering Pulga the shells containing the slippery yolks. Pulga was startled. While he lapped up the raw egg yolks, he decided to think less rashly in the future. His boss should never get the idea that he, Pulga, had something to find fault with.

While they were finishing their meal, the improvised repair job on the radiator had time to dry. Then Gilimon paid for the food and went off to shave. Meanwhile, Pulga dusted off the truck and filled the radiator. He was already sitting in his place when Gilimon climbed up and sat down behind the wheel. They were just about to drive off when Benita appeared in her doorway.

"Gilimon, can you do me a favor?" she called.

"What is it? Speak up."

"Could you take Eduardo along with you a little way down the road?"

"Where to?"

"He is to go and see his grandmother. It is not far."

"All right, if he's ready. I can't wait. Does he have a lot of stuff?"

"Ave María! What could I give him to take along? Just one bag!" Benita shouted plaintively.

"All right then, let's go. Where's the boy?"

Eduardo, who had been hiding behind his mother, was pushed forward.

Pulga moved over, and Eduardo climbed in.

"Be a good boy!" Benita called after him.

In a cloud of dust the truck moved through the wide expanse of countryside. Scorched pastures with great herds of cattle, unending fields of cotton, patches of land where the brown sesame crop already had been gathered in sheaves rolled past them.

The sun rose from the Serranía de Motilones, red and glowing like a ball of fire. A softly timid wind blew across the parched land; the air was heavy and sticky. White cattle stood motionless in the shadows of massive ceibo trees and looked for relief under the rustling roof of palms and foliage along the edges of brooks. Black vultures flew up from a rotting carcass lying by the roadside, then swooped down again when the truck had passed.

The motor hummed with monotonous regularity. The roadway glittered in the oppressive heat. Waves of light seemed to roll over the pavement, which merged with the parched pastureland. Broad treetops and slender palms quivered in the light.

Pulga stared straight ahead, beads of sweat on his face. The blood hummed and pounded in his ears, his tongue clung to his palate, his eyes burned. Before him, over the glitter of white light, an immense expanse of water spread out endlessly. Soft and cool, with indistinct edges merging gradually with the parched plain.

Could that be the ocean, he thought, the ocean that Gilimon had spoken of? He bent forward to see better, but the shiny, glittering surface of water receded slowly as they kept moving. Heat and dust blew into his face. The water, cool and enticing, remained unreachable.

Then he heard Gilimon's voice. "What is that awful stench?"

Pulga was jolted out of his dreams of the ocean, and at that moment he smelled it too. A nauseating almost unbearable smell stung his nostrils. He choked and gulped. "I . . . I don't know."

Eduardo said nothing. He just sat there staring ahead, eyes fixed on the white pavement.

"Virgen Santa, I can't stand it!" Gilimon bent forward and looked all around the little cab where the three were sitting close together on the burning plastic seat. "Is it you?" he asked Eduardo.

Eduardo shook his head. "It must be the cow we saw back there," he murmured.

"The dead cow by the roadside? But that was a long way back. Heavens, it's the stink of rotten meat," Gilimon said slowly. Again he looked around in the cab, and then he saw the bag Eduardo held tightly between his bony knees. "What's in that bag?"

For a second Eduardo looked up at Gilimon, then turned his head forward and continued to stare at the road. "It's for my grandmother," he mumbled.

"What's in it?"

"Nothing."

"Nothing? I want to know what you are taking to your grandmother."

"Nothing," Eduardo repeated.

Gilimon pulled over to the side of the road and stopped. "I think we had better find out." He reached over Pulga's lap and got hold of the bag. With a quick tug he loosened the string and spread the bag open. The penetrating stench of rotten meat hit him. Inside was a piece of greenish pork.

"Heaven forbid!" Gilimon said, swallowing to keep his stomach from turning. "What's that for, boy?"

"That's . . . that's for my grandmother," Eduardo stammered. "That's what my mother gave me to take to my grandmother."

"Virgen Santa, if your grandmother eats that. . . ." He looked at the putrid mess. "Let's get rid of it."

"No, no!" Eduardo exclaimed, scared to death. "My mother will kill me. Her best pig! I must take it to my grandmother. She's sick, the poor woman!"

Eduardo

"I don't think she'll get much better from this," said Gilimon. "Anyway, I don't intend to keep you on my truck with that package of yours. Get out."

Eduardo looked at the unending, blazing road and hesitated. "Couldn't . . . couldn't we put it back on the bags?" he asked, trying to find a way out.

"On my coffee! Virgen Santisima!" Gilimon exclaimed. "Nothing doing. What do you suppose would happen when I got to Barranquilla? Take your stinking mess, and beat it!"

Without a word, his teeth clenched, Eduardo began fumbling at the door handle.

Gilimon looked straight ahead. The road lay straight and white and burning under the sun. Nowhere was there a shadow of shade, and the nearest village was miles away. He could not—damn it!—he simply could not leave the boy here, he thought angrily. "I'll let you come along to the next village. After that you'll be on your own," he said grimly.

Eduardo did not answer. He took the bag from Gilimon's lap and carefully retied the string.

"Hold it out the window," Gilimon ordered. "Otherwise we'll soon be as green as your precious piece of meat."

Eduardo did as he was told. Resignedly he sat there, his skinny arm resting on the frame, his grimy fingers tightly clutching the bag.

They drove on. Under the scorching sun, the bag

outside the window slowly began to drip. The sweetish stench blew in waves through the cab. It did not matter too much; there was no air left in the cab anyway.

When they reached the next village, Gilimon stopped, and Eduardo climbed out silently. His face was expressionless. There was no nod, no word of thanks.

When the truck disappeared around the bend in the road at the other end of the village, he was still standing in the same spot. A confused little figure, upright and hostile, the dripping bag held tightly in his small grimy hand.

11
ON TO FUNDACIÓN

They were approaching Codazzi now, the cotton center, and the traffic on the road grew heavier by the minute. Trucks full of freshly picked cotton dashed past them. Coming from the village were cattle trucks packed with workmen that were being taken to the great cotton plantations. All over the countryside, under the burning sun, they saw men, women, and children, with broad-brimmed straw hats, busily picking cotton.

Codazzi, where they stopped at a filling station, was teeming with life. Through the narrow streets, jeeps and buses, big trucks and pickups, and here and there a passenger car were trying to push on, rumbling and rattling, motors roaring and humming, all horns honking. Outside the coffee shops, workers were sitting in little groups, their families huddled together on the edge of the porches with their bundles and boxes and children, waiting patiently for work.

And still the buses and trucks crammed with men and women and children came pouring into the village, unloading their living cargo in the marketplace, on the narrow streets, outside the eating places and the stores.

"Look at them," said Gilimon, pointing to the groups of people huddled on porch steps, surrounded by their miserable belongings. "I have a notion they all come from Tolima. Of course, it would be just as easy for them to find work nearer home, but they're afraid. They flee from the bandits that roam the countryside back there, ravaging the land with senseless terror and violence."

Pulga nodded. Back in Bogotá more than once he had heard the newsboys shouting about a particularly sensational raid on some isolated plantation or an attack on a busload of people. But he had never given much thought to these things. To him Tolima was just a name, a distant province about

On to Fundación

which his mind was unable to form more than a vague idea.

In Bogotá that kind of trouble was unknown. There no bandits, under the leadership of a Sombra Negra, left a trail of blood and murder behind them. Bogotá had its own problems. And everybody must work out his own difficulties for himself. That was the way Pulga always had thought of distant troubles.

Now he asked, "Do you know Tolima? Do you ever get there?"

"From time to time," Gilimon answered. "I know the whole country. In Medellín or Manizales there is often need of a truck to haul cargo to Bogotá. And then you travel through Tolima, whether it's safe or not."

For a while Pulga hesitated, but then he could no longer resist asking, "Are we going . . . do you think we'll get to drive through Tolima this time?"

Gilimon shrugged. "You never can tell," he answered casually. His thoughts were concentrated on the road again. They passed a dilapidated omnibus with a flat tire and honked their way through the anthill of passengers surrounding the bus. Then they had to swing around a truck standing in the middle of the road with a broken axle. The driver lay asleep in the shade under the truck.

"Finally a man with horse sense," Gilimon observed approvingly. A loud, long yawn came from deep inside him.

They had passed through Codazzi and were now approaching Valledupar on a road that had a hard surface and was kept in better repair. Faster vehicles now overtook them more readily, but the dust was less of a nuisance. They, too, were making better time. The truck rolled smoothly, the tires sang, the motor hummed in unbroken monotony.

Now that Eduardo was no longer sitting next to him, Pulga had more room in the cab. He could catch the current of air, hot though it was, coming in through the open side window. And the stench was gone.

"It's a good thing we got rid of that boy with his stinking bag," he said.

There was no answer.

The truck was in the center of the road, far to the left, cutting into the oncoming lane. Behind them Pulga heard impatient honking, impatient and getting more insistent.

"What's the hurry in this heat?" said Pulga with an undertone of aggressive disapproval.

Again there was no response. He turned halfway around and saw that Gilimon's head was bent forward, his chin touching his chest, his mouth half

On to Fundación

open. The truck swerved more and more to the left into the oncoming traffic lane.

"Boss, boss," Pulga warned. And then, frightened and totally confused, he shouted, "Gilimon!"

Gilimon awoke. Clutching the steering wheel, he regained control of the truck and swerved back into the right lane. The bus behind them rushed past, with the driver leaning on his horn. His helper, standing on the running board, leaned over, spouting a torrent of curses and abuse in the general direction of Gilimon.

Staring forlornly at the bus with the high-strung, wound-up helper, whose fury almost toppled him off the running board, Gilimon tried to appear as though none of this had anything to do with him. He moved back more firmly in his seat, passed his hand several times across his forehead, and produced a bottle of *aguardiente* from within the folds of his *ruana*, which was lying next to him.

Now in full control of the truck, Gilimon took a sturdy draft and then another. He sighed and handed the bottle over to Pulga. "Here, screw the top on. Lucky thing you didn't doze off, too."

Pulga blushed to his ears. Never before had anyone praised him. And now here was Gilimon. . . . Embarrassed, he looked outside. In order to get hold of himself, he began to count the cars coming from the opposite direction. At the same time he watched lest they were drifting again to the left side of the road. He almost hoped they would! Now and again he glanced stealthily at Gilimon, to see whether he was still awake. Like a small watchdog, he sat on the edge of his seat looking out for his boss and the truck.

The *aguardiente* had helped, and Gilimon was again fully awake. From the corner of his eye he looked at his little helper. Pulga, however, was too busy to notice.

In the distance a vague form loomed up in the vast emptiness over the horizon, a grayish-blue shadow that increased in size as they drove on. "We're not far from Valledupar," Gilimon said and sighed. "That over there is the Sierra Nevada de Santa Marta."

A few minutes later they drove through the wretched little town at the foot of the mighty mountain. Just outside the town, Gilimon pulled up in front of an untidy-looking eating place by the roadside. In the shade on the wooden porch they ordered their midday meal.

On the railing along the porch a sickly-looking monkey full of bald spots was running about, tied to a rope. In a sandy plot in front of the building a parrot was sitting on a pole talking shrilly to the customers. Aside from Gilimon and Pulga, there

On to Fundación

was only one gentleman and his little boy, drinking lemonade under a parasol in the open lot.

In spite of the heat, the little boy was running about, from the table to the monkey, to the parrot, and back again to the table. When his father, having gone off to their car, called him, he reluctantly took leave of the monkey and the parrot and skipped across the lot to where the car was waiting.

Pulga noticed that the little boy, with all his jumping around, had lost his pocketknife, which had fallen noiselessly into the loose sand. The slovenly waiter, his dirty thumb in the soup plate he was shoving across their table, also saw the knife fall. Casually he walked over to the spot. Strolling back and forth, he managed to push some sand over the knife and began to collect the empty lemonade bottles. With a dirty towel he wiped the table laboriously, until the car was out of sight. Then he bent down, picked up the knife, and dropped it into one of his pockets.

Looking over the edge of his soup plate, Pulga had watched the performance step by step with concentrated interest. He could not help grinning in admiration. The whole thing had been handled very smoothly. Not once had the slow fellow taken a faster step, not a muscle in his face had moved in any unusual way. Nothing in his behavior could have given him away. A smooth job, indeed.

PULGA

Gilimon's voice called Pulga out of his reverie. "All set? Let's go. Why are you sitting there, grinning like an idiot?"

Pulga wisely refrained from explaining the cause of his amusement. Hurriedly he gulped down the last spoonfuls of soup and jumped up. As they drove off the empty lot, he turned back, trying to catch the waiter's eye. But the waiter was leaning against the rail of the veranda, teasing the mangy old monkey with his dish towel. The soiled soup plates and empty beer bottles remained where Gilimon and Pulga had left them.

Outside Valledupar, nothing was left of the hard road top. In a cloud of dust they drove along the narrow winding road at the foot of the sierra with its towering, snow-covered peaks. The avocado and mango trees were gray with dust; the coconut and date palms trembled in the heat. The sun beat down on the tobacco plants, the yucca, the broad leaves of the banana plants. Scorched dry, the softly undulating grassland stretched out toward the west as far as the eye could see, merging with marshlands and lakes and the broad, gray Magdalena River. To their right they still had the fantastic slope of the gigantic, snow-topped mountain, an isolated towering mass in the hot coastal plain.

They drove on till daylight began to wane, and the folds and ravines in the towering walls of rock vanished under black shadows. A chilly gray fog descended from the clouds that hid the snow-covered mountain tops. It began to drizzle.

By the time they reached the village of Fundación, the drizzle had turned into heavy rain. Gilimon stopped in front of a small hotel where other trucks were parked under the heavy mango trees. A yellow light shone from the open door and between the slats of the window shutters. Loud voices and laughter could be heard from inside the taproom.

"That's it," said Gilimon climbing down from his seat. "We're going to spend the night here. It's time that I get the feel of a mattress under my back for a change."

But it was not that simple. The taproom was filled with salesmen, cattle buyers, and truck drivers. Only the billiard table or the wooden bench in the corner was left for Gilimon, but the men were glad to move over and make room for him at the large round table laden with bottles of beer and *aguardiente*.

After supper Pulga went back to the truck. From the dark cab he could look straight into the taproom and hear everything the men were saying. The numbers of bottles on the table kept increasing by the minute, and the voices grew louder. Pulga could follow the conversation almost word for word:

A truck had rolled off the ferry across the Magdalena River. The driver had managed to escape, but the cargo was lost and the helper drowned. A few kilometers downstream his body had been fished out of the water.

Oh, well, there was a man who had nothing to worry about anymore.

They say that when you drown, you see your whole life flash through your mind. Not a pleasant thing, come to think of it.

True. But even so, drowning wasn't the worst kind of death. At least you did not die of thirst. . . .

Like that fellow in the Guajira. If ever there was a narrow escape, that was it.

What story was that?

Oh, a fellow with a pickup had lost his way in the Guajira. He had been traveling around and around in a circle until he ran out of gasoline. That could easily happen in the parched land east of the big mountain, a godforsaken country at the far end of the world. A hard barren plain with each tall, straight, powerful cactus resembling the next one. Of course, the man had no one to blame but himself. He had undertaken his trip without a guide. Back in Ríohacha they had warned him time and again, but he went by himself anyway.

"Must have been a gringo," said someone. "They think they know everything."

By pure luck a couple of Guajira Indians had

finally found him, two women with their faces blackened with plant juices. He was still alive. Half dead, but still alive. He had drunk the water from the radiator and gone to lie down under the pickup in the shade. A good thing he had not left his truck, trying to walk it. A good thing they finally found him. That is what is called luck, for sure.

Gilimon—to everybody's delight—told the story of Eduardo with his bagful of dripping meat.

Pulga heard them laugh. He heard the raindrops tapping on the foliage of the mango trees, on the metal roof of the cab. His eyelids were heavy.

From far away came the rushing of a mountain stream along the dark slope of the great mountain. White, gushing, ice-cold water from the eerie, snow-covered heights of the Sierra Nevada.

12

THE FERRY ACROSS THE MAGDALENA RIVER

"You, Pulga," said Gilimon, "climb up and sit on top of our freight. Make sure you don't fall off. I'm not going to go back looking for you."

The two men whom they had picked up in Cienaga, where they had eaten fish and yucca and baked bananas for breakfast, already were seated in the cab. They were to come along all the way to the ferry across the Magdalena River. A companion of theirs, who carried a string of fish, was left behind wisely by Gilimon in Cienaga.

The road between the ocean and the large land-

The Ferry Across the Magdalena River

locked lake, the Cienaga Grande, was wide and straight. Pulga kept looking out over the ocean, as though he wanted to make quite certain that what he saw was real. Long bluish waves came rolling up over the sandy beach, forming white crests of foam, then receded, making room for the next swell.

On the other side, over the tops of the mangroves, he could see the vast expanse of the Cienaga Grande, a seemingly unending bluish-green lake, merging in the green of its shores. On the lee side of the dark mangrove islands the water was calm and smooth like a mirror. Farther out the wind gently rippled its surface. Small fishing vessels with triangular sails moved between the islands, coming over the horizon like white butterflies. The round fishing nets were cast out, hovered for a moment above the surface of the water, then disappeared from sight.

It was hard for Pulga to decide what to look at first in this new world. There he was sitting up on top of the truck, high and mighty and proud. The wide roadbed zoomed along far beneath him, squeezed between the two vast bodies of water, straight like a pencil line drawn on paper with a ruler.

He looked back over his shoulder at the fishing village of Cienaga in a setting of palm trees. Rising high above the fishermen's plain huts, the snow-covered peak of the Sierra Nevada was etched with the finest of needles against the azure tropical sky. Clean and unapproachable in its glistening grandeur, the solitary mountain with its white peak stood there, proud and aloof, as though it were challenging the fierce sun of the tropics. Below the snow line blue shadows passed over into the darker violet of the ravines and gullies. Naked walls of purple rock rose up from the gently undulating green pasture land and the blue ocean.

On and on they drove along the edge of the water, the tires humming evenly over the pavement. Pulga's long untidy hair flapped about his ears. The salt wind blew through the holes in his shirt. Steadily they approached Barranquilla, the harbor at the mouth of the Magdalena River, and now Pulga saw the vague skyline of the city in the haze above the broad expanse of water.

Gilimon slowed down, and then stopped at the pier of the ferry. Like a small monkey, Pulga slid off his perch on top of the cargo. He was down on the ground before Gilimon had climbed out of the cab. The two passengers settled their accounts, thanked them, and disappeared into the crowd.

Pulga looked around. A long row of vehicles— passenger cars, jeeps, pickups, freight trucks—was lined up on the pier waiting for the ferry. Women

and children with huge baskets of food and sweets milled around the waiting cars.

"*Pan de yucca, pan de yucca!*" they shouted. "*Bocadilloooos, chicheron, empañada, chicheron!*" The noise was ear-splitting.

They held up their baskets with fresh yucca rolls, thick sweet fruit jelly wrapped in leaves, and crisply baked hog skin. Through the car windows they thrust chunks of fat meat and fried chicken right under the noses of the perspiring travelers. "Fried chicken, hog skin, hard-boiled eggs, baked fish! Fresh, everything fresh!" voices shrieked in praise of their wares.

A small boy with a stick of yucca rings over his shoulder walked along the row of cars. A tall fellow, whose emaciated face bore all the features of a professional bum, used his nimble, bony fingers to remove a few rings from the stick without attracting the boy's attention. Nonchalantly, he ambled down along the row of waiting cars.

"Yucca, yucca, yucca," sang the boy's metallic voice.

A Negro woman waddled along with a tray full of peeled hard-boiled eggs and pieces of fat chicken balanced on the palm of her hand at shoulder height. A young fellow, who had come stumbling out of a bar on unsteady legs, tried to make his way past her. The tray landed on the ground, and the pieces of chicken and the eggs scattered in all directions. The black woman began to scold and curse, and as the young man fled, her curses became louder and more expressive. Finally she bent down, picked up her tray, wiped the pieces of chicken and the eggs on her apron, and proceeded on her appointed course.

Outside one of the wretched eating places, where chunks of meat were roasting over charcoal fires, and pitchers of fruit juice and bottles of beer and *aguardiente* stood ready on shaky tables, a giant of a man waved his powerful arms. "Gilimo-o-n," he called. "Gilimo-o-n, what a pleasure to see you! What a small world!"

Gilimon's face lit up. "There's Polidorio so help me," he said. "You watch out for the truck, Pulga. I'll be back in no time."

Gilimon hurried across to Polidorio's table. They slapped each other on the shoulders and back, and Polidorio boomed out an order for more beer.

In the cab the heat was oppressive. Pulga stayed outside, leaning against the half-open door. Along the row of cars he could see the broad grayish expanse of the Magdalena River. The heavy, clumsy ferryboat slowly approached from the other side. A canoe flitted past. A tugboat pushed a group of heavily loaded barges upriver; black masses of smoke from its two smokestacks hung over the water. Clusters of purple water hyacinths drifted seaward.

Suddenly Pulga straightened up. Something was moving outside the door on the other side of the truck. Someone was leaning against the cab, the same fellow who had helped himself to the yucca rings only a few minutes ago. His bony fingers were resting casually on the frame of the open window. The hand slid down; the fingers wiggled over the seat toward Gilimon's *ruana*.

Pulga watched dumbfounded. What was he to do? Should he call out? But the fellow certainly would deny Pulga's accusation indignantly and make him swallow his words. Where was Gilimon? The wriggling fingers were gathering together the folds of the *ruana*, and the hand seemed ready to snatch it away.

There was not a second to spare. Pulga slid into the cab like a snake, his belly gliding over the hot seat. He bared his teeth and sank them with a snap into the skinny fingers till he hit bone. With a piercing scream and a most uninhibited curse, the man fled. Clutching the *ruana* to his body, Pulga slid down to the floor of the cab and remained there curled up tightly. He heard the man still shouting and cursing, but did not have the heart to sit up. Then the revving, the hissing and coughing, the purring and rolling of motors being started drowned out all other noises. The ferryboat had arrived, and the drivers happily honked their horns as the vehicles began to roll off onto the pier.

Gilimon came back to his truck on the double. As he yanked the door open and jumped in, he barely missed stepping on Pulga. "What are you doing down there? Get up! Put my *ruana* back where it belongs. I can't even reach the gas pedal. What were you up to?"

He did not wait for an answer.

"I just hope we'll get on," said Gilimon anxiously, sticking his head out the window, as the long line of waiting cars began to move slowly.

"You better keep that stinking dog of yours on a leash," snarled an angry voice. But Gilimon paid no attention to the tall, slim man who appeared alongside his window, licking his fingers, glaring furiously.

They drove across onto the ferryboat. "Look out, make sure we fit!" Gilimon shouted to Pulga. His warning was quite unnecessary; Pulga was leaning so far out of his window that he almost lost his balance.

Slowly they moved across the wide river. Pulga sat erect and still, eyes wide open, staring at the whirling mass of muddy water. The heavily laden ferryboat bobbed gently up and down, and Pulga's fingers held on desperately to the window frame.

The Ferry Across the Magdalena River

What if the boat were to capsize? What if the truck were to slide off? They would go down like a brick. They would disappear forever in the dirty grayish water. Ave María, how had he gotten into this?

He watched in utter amazement when Polidorio cooly climbed out of his green truck and came walking across to chat with Gilimon through the open side window.

"Is . . . is that the captain?" Pulga stuttered, when he saw a man with a wooden leg stomping about, making his way in between the cars and trucks on board. Every time he set down his wooden leg Pulga had the feeling that the ferryboat would turn over, and in sheer misery he felt the fish and the yucca move in his stomach.

"No, the captain is standing up there," Polidorio answered. He looked at Pulga's scared face and added with a comforting chuckle, "This fellow here shows the drivers where there's still a space they can squeeze into. The old fox knows precisely how he must arrange the cars and trucks in order to get the greatest possible number on the ferry without too much risk of sinking."

"But . . . but he's thumping so hard . . . he has only one leg," Pulga said worriedly.

"So much the better—he weighs less," Polidorio answered airily. He gave Pulga an encouraging smile, talked to Gilimon about getting together in

Barranquilla, and ambled back to his huge shiny truck.

Pulga was silent throughout the rest of their journey. His voice came back to him only after they had left the rolling, bobbing ferryboat and were driving on their way to Barranquilla. Only then did he tell his boss about the miserable crook who had tried to steal Gilimon's *ruana* and whose hand he, Pulga, had bitten.

"So that's why you were lying all crumpled up under the seat, and why that fellow at the ferry was shouting something about a dog," said Gilimon. "Who would have thought of that?" He burst out laughing and Pulga merrily chimed in.

And so they drove into Barranquilla.

13

PULGA'S TENNIS SHOES

The city was burning hot. The air over the asphalt trembled, and a cloud of dust hung over the houses.

They delivered their coffee and went to see several forwarding agents. Finally they tracked down a truckload of cement for delivery to Montería, but the man at the agent's office refused to make a definite promise. He did not know whether he could reach his client that same day; possibly they would have to wait till the following morning. He suggested they come back later in the afternoon.

Gilimon and Pulga drove the truck to a repair

shop to get the radiator fixed and the motor tuned up.

"Now let's go and see where we can find something to eat," said Gilimon, as they headed back in the scorching heat toward the center of town.

"What's that peculiar way of walking, Pulga?" asked Gilimon after a while, slightly annoyed. "Are you a cripple or something? What's come over you? Have you become such a gentleman that you can't use your legs anymore?"

"The pavement is so hot," Pulga confessed meekly. "I get stuck in the asphalt. My feet are getting burned."

Gilimon looked down at Pulga's feet. Between the dirty toes oozed a soft paste of asphalt. Gilimon burst out laughing, and Pulga looked very unhappy. "In that case we'd better go and buy you a pair of shoes," said Gilimon. "Come along and don't look so scared. I'm going to pay for your shoes. After all, if I had to buy a new *ruana*, it would cost more."

They went into a shop that sold clothes, toys, tableware, painted shells, and also shoes.

Pulga could hardly understand what was going on. Never before had he walked into this kind of store without someone's screaming at him and chasing him out. A swarthy salesgirl appeared from the rear, asked what they were looking for, and directed them, without concealing her boredom, to where the shoes were displayed.

"Well," said Gilimon, "say something."

But Pulga was speechless, completely bewildered. Finally he pointed hesitatingly to a pair of white tennis shoes.

"Those?" Gilimon asked.

Pulga nodded.

"They'll be dirty in no time, you know. Shouldn't you take another color?"

Pulga shook his head and again pointed to the white tennis shoes.

"All right then," said Gilimon. "If those are what you want, those it shall be. The decision is yours."

Once outside, Pulga scarcely dared put down his feet. Walking carefully, as though on a surface of glass, he kept looking at his shiny shoes and narrowly escaped being run over by a passing car.

Gilimon was becoming impatient. "Wake up!" he snapped. "Look where you're going. Or do you think we have nothing else to do all day but admire your shoes? It's time for us to get something to eat. Then we have to get back to the freight office, and I also want to check at the repair shop to see if they've done any work on our truck." He added resignedly, "I'm afraid not. The mechanics around here seem to get tired from just thinking of work."

Gilimon knew what he was talking about. When

later in the afternoon they returned to the repair shop, the truck was still standing where they had left it.

As Gilimon was telling the men what he thought of their service, Polidorio drove up in his truck. "Gilimon, why get excited!" he shouted. "Isn't it hot enough already? That truck of yours will be ready by the time the sun rises again. Let your helper stay here and keep an eye on what's being done, and you come along with me. I'm on my way downtown to rinse some of the dust out of my gullet."

Taking hold of Gilimon's arm, he pulled him away, and they disappeared into the crowd, each carrying his little suitcase.

Pulga faithfully kept an eye on the work, watching what the mechanics were doing under the hood step by step. When he got his nose too close to theirs, though, he was chased away or snarled at. One thing was certain: Gilimon's words had made an impression. The truck got a thorough checkup.

Pulga crept back into the cab and began once again to examine his shoes. He passed his fingers over the coarsely woven material, moistened his index finger with his tongue to remove a spot on the rubber tip, and with his fingernails began to poke the dirt out of the deep grooves in the soles.

By the time Pulga was through with this job, it was getting dark. Meanwhile, the mechanics had

Pulga's Tennis Shoes

finished their work on the truck. The doors of the shop were locked, and the workmen gradually left for home. The lot where the truck was parked was almost vacant.

Street lights and neon signs were switched on, and music blared out of bars and eating places. Honking automobiles moved through the narrow streets. From Bocas de Ceniza, the sandy bay outside the harbor, came the whistling signals of the water traffic. Crowds of people were milling outside store windows, and the coffee shops were filled to capacity. The hot city was seething with life.

Pulga stretched out on the seat, hands under his head, heels resting on the frame of the side window. In this position, peering through his lashes, he could see his feet clearly. The shoes caught the light of a street lamp. They were white and shiny. He could not take his eyes off his shoes. He had earned them! Ave María, life was good. And so full of unexpected happenings. Who could have imagined all this that night when he had crept under a truck to keep out of the rain? In Bogotá it was probably raining right now. Had Tío Pepe come yet to take Pedro on his begging expedition in the cold outside the movie houses? Here in the cab it was roasting hot.

In the small hidden valley at Mamá Marjua's . . . that was nice! Pedro would have liked it there, too, in the sun near the waterfall, with the wind blowing through the pine trees. Oh, well, he couldn't have everything. Tomorrow morning they would travel on to take a load of cement to . . . to. . . . What was the name of that place? His lids were heavy. Pulga closed his eyes and slept.

When he awoke, it was already light, but Gilimon had not yet turned up. Slowly Pulga rubbed his eyes. Vaguely he remembered that there was something . . . something special. Of course! His face lit up. How could he have forgotten! He lifted his head to look at his feet. Slowly he raised his body and stared. He stretched out his hand and touched his feet.

It could not be true! No, it could not be!

Once again he passed his fingertips over his dirty, bare feet with their black, broken toenails. He moved across the seat, opened the door, and searched the ground. He looked all around the truck, under it, inside the cab. Again he walked around the truck, again he searched inside it, front and back. Nothing was there.

He stared down at his naked feet. "My shoes!" he screamed. "My shoes! Where are my shoes!"

"Why are you standing there howling and carrying on?" asked the night watchman, half asleep, as he dragged himself across the lot toward the truck. "What are you doing here anyway? Get going!"

But Pulga did not hear him. He sat down on the running board, hiding his head in his arms. His shoulders began to shake.

Pulga cried and cried. He wept as though his heart were breaking.

14

JAIME'S FAMILY
Barranquilla to Copacabana

The land was dry, the hills scorched red. Jeeps and buses overtaking them on the smouldering road from Barranquilla to Cartagena whirled up dense clouds of dust. Men sitting with crossed legs on donkeys, old women bent under the weight of bundles of kindling wood, or driving herds of goats, loomed up in the lingering dust and vanished again.

Now and then a group of stray donkeys broke out from the underbrush, crossing the road several car lengths ahead of them. Whenever they appeared, Gilimon applied his brakes, but the movement was automatic. He no longer had the energy to curse at the dumb beasts. Listlessly he sat behind the wheel, his head buzzing, his eyes burning, his throat parched.

That morning, when he finally had returned to his truck, he was in a rosy mood, happily humming a catching tune. His head was brimful of jukebox music, and on his tongue still lingered the taste of *aguardiente*. They had had a grand time, Polidorio and he. A man needed a change once in a while from the fog and cold, the dust and heat of the road. And Polidorio was quite a fellow—nobody like him!

Then Gilimon had discovered his helper, huddled on the running board, crying his heart out. Bit by bit, through Pulga's incoherent stammering, he had pieced together the story of the stolen shoes. At first Gilimon had burst out laughing, but then he felt sorry for the boy and tried to cheer him up. Oh, yes, shoes were like that, always causing trouble. The same thing had happened to him once when he spent a night in jail, through no fault of his own. During the night someone stole his shoes, and the following day there was nothing he could do but walk away in his socks.

But no matter what Gilimon had said, nothing seemed to help, and finally he got fed up with Pulga's sniveling. He had pulled him away from the running board and told him to snap out of it. They were here because there was a job to be done. They had to pick up that load of cement, and they had a ride ahead of them.

Pulga had swallowed his tears, but his heart was not in his work. He sat quietly next to Gilimon and stared at the desperately dried-out countryside with its cactuses and scorched brush growth. From time to time he cast a stealthy glance at his dangling bare feet.

Miserable, wretched. . . . Pulga could think of no word to fit the scoundrel who had played such a despicable trick on him. Those had been his shoes, his property. Shoes were not given to him every day. He had done his best. He had earned them.

For the first time in his life Pulga could not resign himself to accepting what came to him. He always had let events take their course, without resistance, always been ready to submit, always the victim. He took it for granted that he must adjust to circumstances as they occurred. Now, for the first time, he found himself in revolt against fate. In the course of his journey with Gilimon something had awakened in him. A vague awareness of his own worth, a dim notion that he was good for something, that he could be of use.

The discovery was bewildering. It had produced the budding of a strange and unknown desire. Blurred, uncertain, hardly conscious, hope had arisen

Jaime's Family

for a better life, an existence worthy of a human being.

In Pulga's chaotic world, the tennis shoes had been something tangible. His first, brand-new possession —straight from the store—they were the symbol of all his awakening feelings. And they had been taken away from him.

By the time they had passed Cartagena, neither Gilimon nor Pulga had spoken a word. Finally Gilimon stopped at a gas station. Taking advantage of a barrel of water, he doused his head, and Pulga followed his example. While they were washing, a thin, undersized man sauntered up to the truck. At first he watched them with great interest, then walked around the truck, thoughtfully examining the freight bed, only a quarter of which was filled with cement bags. He followed Gilimon and Pulga to a little snack bar across the road, where Gilimon ordered something to eat and a lemonade for himself and Pulga.

Pulga had been watching the unobtrusive, little man for quite a while. Now he moved toward him for a closer view of the wretched fellow, who looked cornered and hopeless.

As though Pulga's movement were an invitation, the man tried to start a conversation. "To Medellín?" he asked Gilimon.

"To Montería," Gilimon answered.

"I see, to Montería! That means not to Medellín."

"No, to Montería."

"With cement?"

"Yes, with cement."

"Care for a beer?" offered the little fellow.

Gilimon shook his head. "I'm going to stick to my lemonade."

The man hesitated and then said, "The thing is, I was working at a *finca* a little way down the road."

Gilimon looked uninterested.

"The work was good. The wages were good. The boss treated me well. . . ." The man fell silent and looked at Gilimon. "The thing is," he began again when Gilimon did not reply, "I was satisfied, they treated me well. But my wife does not want to stay here." He looked quite unhappy. "My wife does not want to stay here," he repeated. "The son of the boss bothers her, she says."

"Is that so?" Gilimon replied. "Well, that happens in the best of families."

"Now she wants to go back to Antioquia. That is where we come from. We come from near Medellín—this side of Medellín. And now she wants to go back. Every night, she says, she sees the son of the boss. That is to say, the former boss."

The little man stared outside and shook his head. "It's been more than twenty years now, but he keeps coming back every night. He wanders about the house and all through the stables and servants' quarters. And then he stands in the shadow of the big mango tree. That is where it happened, they say around here. That is where he was killed with a machete. He goes back there every night, looking for his hand, they say. My wife says so, too. She herself has seen him. It gives her the creeps, and she does not want to stay any longer. She has packed her things and wants to go back to Antioquia, this side of Medellín. I thought, since you go in that direction anyway with a half-empty truck, you might perhaps take us along—for a fee, of course. . . ."

"But we're not going to Medellín. We're going to Montería," Gilimon objected.

"I thought, once we are under way," the man persisted, "somewhere around Sincelejo, I mean, we should be able to get transportation from there for the rest of the journey." From one of his pockets he produced a badly worn purse. "I have money. I can pay. Just tell me what you will charge. I'll be glad to let you have a down payment, too." His voice sounded as though he were about to break into tears.

Gilimon shrugged his shoulders. "All right then, get going," he said. "But don't think I'm going to drive up to some godforsaken dirt road to that *finca* of yours. I'll be damned if I do. In that case you can just stay where you are."

"My wife is sitting all ready by the roadside," the man said quickly. "She sits there and waits." He nodded enthusiastically, happy to have made arrangements after all.

They agreed on a price and started out. Some distance down the road, where a path branched off through a gate to a large hacienda, sat a large, sinewy woman surrounded by a swarm of children, a dog, a goat, a crate of chickens, and various ramshackle housekeeping equipment.

"This is it," said the little man.

Gilimon stopped the truck and looked in astonishment at the display by the side of the road. "Is that it?" he asked. He pointed to the group of eleven children, who had stopped playing and now stood staring at the big truck. "All these are yours?"

The man looked the children over thoughtfully, as though seeing them for the first time. "*Pues*, well, that's what they are. Mine," he conceded slowly. "And the baby, too." He pointed to his wife, who was nursing a child, surrounded by the dog, the goat, and the chickens.

"But listen, old one, that's not what we agreed on. If I had known that you had such a crowd. . . ."

The little man raised his shoulders and looked

resigned. "*Pues*, what can I do? Is it my fault that marriage has its consequences?"

Now the woman spoke. "Jaime!" she snapped. "How much longer do you want me and this pitiful flock to sit in the sun?"

The man found it difficult to hide his nervousness. "Yes, yes, be patient, be patient," he mumbled. Like a hunted animal, he looked shyly and hopefully at Gilimon.

"In that case you will have to add a little something to the price we agreed on," Gilimon said coolly. "But the goat cannot come along. He'll damage the cargo."

"But . . . but," Jaime sputtered.

"Take it or leave it. It's all the same to me," said Gilimon laconically.

Quickly Jaime changed tactics. "All right, all right, if it can't be done otherwise," he said meekly, and began ordering his children to put their belongings on the truck. A table, chairs, hammocks, pots and pans, the crate of chickens, the dog, and the children were stowed away next to and on top of the cement bags. Jaime and his wife, with the baby in her arms, climbed in last. The goat, bleating pitifully, stayed behind.

"It surely looks like a moving van," Gilimon observed, without trying to conceal his annoyance.

They drove on for a long time, but did not reach

Sincelejo. When it got dark, Gilimon pulled up by the roadside. "I've had it," he said. "All I care about now is sleep."

He hung a few pieces of newspaper over the cab windows and rested his head on his folded arms over the steering wheel, as he was accustomed to doing. In no time he was fast asleep.

Pulga moved into his corner of the cab. For a while he listened to the carping and wailing in back where eleven children were busy pushing each other around, and Jaime and his wife were quarreling, and the baby was whining. All that he had been through in the course of that day had exhausted him. Finally Pulga, too, sank into a deep and heavy sleep, from which he awoke with a sudden shock.

Gray light filtered through the newspapers. Outside and inside everything was quiet. But something had awakened him. What was it?

Cautiously he opened the cab door and as he climbed out into the hazy morning, he saw a shadow disappear into the undergrowth alongside the road, not far behind the truck. Puzzled, he stared at the spot; then instantly he saw the light. He walked to the back of the truck and peered inside. Nothing was there except the bags of cement, and some of those appeared to be missing.

Pulga yanked open the other cab door and awakened Gilimon. "They're gone!" he whispered ur-

Jaime's Family

gently. "But I think I know where they're hiding. Just over here . . . come quickly. They took a couple of bags of cement with them."

Gilimon, still half asleep, did not grasp what Pulga was saying right away, but once fully awake he reached the growth of bushes in back of the truck with a few determined steps.

Underneath, hidden away in a ditch, sat Jaime with his flock of children, his livestock, and the rest of his belongings. His wife with the baby in her arms sat enthroned on the bags of cement.

"What's going on here?" Gilimon asked roughly.

Jaime looked up in innocent surprise. "What do you mean, *señor*?"

"What I mean," Gilimon said coldly, "is that you and yours were trying to make your getaway without paying your debt. And, what's more, you stole part of my freight."

Jaime was at a loss for an answer; he looked bewildered and miserable. Now his wife offered her contribution to the dispute. "Part of his freight? He called that part of his freight—two puny bags of cement!" she shouted contemptuously. "And what about my goat? We had to leave it behind. Think of all the money we lost! And now this swindler wants us to pay him. We are not in Sincelejo yet, and already he insists on his money!"

Gilimon did not waste many more words on Jaime

and his family. He collared two of the oldest boys and ordered them to carry the bags of cement back to the truck and to put them down exactly where they had been stacked.

As they drove off, they could hear the woman raving indignantly about her goat.

15

THE WAKE FOR MENARDO

Montería was a quiet town, surrounded by cotton fields and huge estates. Gilimon and Pulga delivered their load of cement there, but did not find another cargo.

"You may want to try at Las Palmas," a man said finally in the coffee shop where Gilimon and Pulga sat down to drink *un refajo,* a mixture of beer and lemonade.

"At Las Palmas?" Gilimon repeated.

"Yes, it's some fifty to sixty kilometers from here, a very large hacienda, not far from Planeta Rica.

Anybody in that part of the country can tell you where it is. They sold some cattle to Copacabana, just this side of Medellín, and the stock has to go either today or tomorrow."

"But I'm not equipped to transport cows," Gilimon answered.

The man shrugged his shoulders. "What of it? They can fix that with bamboo sticks and some straw," he said casually, then got up and left without paying for his beer.

Gilimon picked up the tab. A good tip was worth a little something.

He tried a few more places, for the idea of having cows in his truck did not appeal to him. But there seemed to be no freight anywhere in Montería, and toward noon they drove on in the direction of Planeta Rica to Las Palmas.

The hacienda, far inland, was surrounded by cotton and rice fields and gentle hills, where the cattle were pastured. The low, white mansion with its overhanging tile roof and spacious verandas lay tucked away among blooming shrubs and tall waving palm trees.

The big yard was deserted except for an old woman, busily making flat cake from yucca meal on a table outside one of the cottages. She barely looked up when the truck drove into the yard.

Gilimon honked his horn a few times, and when

that brought no response he got out and walked over to the woman. "I've been told you have cattle here that need to be taken somewhere."

The little woman pulled her shoulders up and the corners of her mouth down. "Hard to tell," she said, and continued to knead and roll her thin cakes.

"Is the foreman around?"

"The foreman?" the woman repeated thoughtfully. "If Don Antonio is the man you mean, Antonio Vejardo. . . ."

"Yes, he's the one," said Gilimon, taking a chance.

"Well, he would be out in the fields, or maybe with the heifers in back of Don Silencio's cottage. You know, he's our top cattleman. If that's where he is, it will take awhile for him to get here."

Gilimon walked back to his truck and stood around for a while with Pulga, trying to make up his mind. Then a man on a small, spirited horse came riding across the yard.

"That's Don Antonio," the woman called out to Gilimon. "Did I not tell you he would be here in a moment?"

The man on horseback rode over to the truck and greeted Gilimon.

"I was told back in Montería that you have cattle here to go to Medellín," Gilimon said.

Antonio nodded. "Yes, to Copacabana," he said. "That's this side of Medellín."

"Sure," Gilimon agreed, slightly vexed. He did not have to be told where Copacabana was.

Antonio looked the truck over. "It isn't a cattle truck, I see," he said slowly.

"In Montería I was told that would be no problem, but if you think otherwise. . . . For me the idea of getting my truck full of cow manure is not so terribly attractive either. In that case, we'd better go." Gilimon got ready to climb back into the cab.

"Wait a second," said Antonio quickly. "Let's walk over to Don Roque—he's the owner of the hacienda—and find out what his thinking is in this matter. After all, we do have straw and bamboo to take care of that little problem. It's a fine, sturdy vehicle you have there."

"It sure is!" said Gilimon without trying to conceal his pride. He motioned to Pulga to stay with the truck and followed Antonio up to the mansion, where Don Roque was enjoying his siesta in a hammock on one of the verandas.

In the bushes between the clusters of bamboo along the edge of the yard, Pulga heard a rustling noise. Then he saw branches and leaves pushed aside, and a boy appeared.

When he saw Pulga, he called out, "Have you see my father anywhere? Where is he?"

Pulga shrugged. "How should I know?"

"My father is the foreman around here," the boy explained.

"Oh, him. He walked up that way with my boss." Pulga pointed toward the mansion. "They went to talk to Don Roque."

The boy came closer. He brushed the back of his hand over his mouth and said, "He has breathed his last. I just came from there."

"Who?" asked Pulga, taken aback. "Don Roque is . . . ?"

"Don Roque . . . are you mad? *That* would be something up here."

"But who are you talking about?"

"Old Menardo, of course. Right away they put him on the table Tomasa uses to knead her yucca dough. Tomasa is his wife. She has almost lost her mind. She just sits there and carries on. But what's the use of that!" The boy raised his shoulders in resignation. "She saw it coming. He no longer ate anything—no yucca cake, no beans, no *mazamorra*. There was nothing left of him but bones and skin. He's all shriveled up like a lizard. Come on, I'll show you."

For a moment Pulga hesitated. To see Menardo lying on the yucca-cake table, looking like a lizard —that was something! But there was the truck and Gilimon's suitcase in the cab. He shook his head.

"I must watch the truck till my boss comes back," he said with a touch of regret in his voice.

"Oh, are you the helper?"

Pulga nodded proudly. "Yes, that's what I am."

"What's your name?"

"Pulga."

"Oh, mine is Antonio, just like my father's, but they call me Tonio. What did you come here for?"

"To pick up cattle for Medellín."

"I suppose you mean Copacabana," Tonio corrected, obviously pleased with himself for having such detailed information. "They'll have to go and get the cattle. They didn't know you were coming."

Pulga agreed that he and his boss had arrived without warning.

"In that case you'll leave tomorrow," Tonio predicted. "It's quite late now, and the young cattle are out in the hills far beyond the cow sheds where Silencio lives. He's our chief cattleman. His cottage is all the way back there. You can't see it from here, but that's where it is." Tonio made a broad sweep with his arm.

"Tomorrow we'll have the funeral, and tonight is the wake," he added without pausing.

"What?"

"Menardo's burial," Tonio explained, somewhat impatiently. "And then there will be the nine days of mourning." He nodded enthusiastically. Obviously he was looking forward to the nine days when all of them would be gathered at Menardo's house as Tomasa's guests. She was going to have to slaughter a young pig in order to have something to eat for everyone. That much was certain. And beer and *aguardiente* would flow freely.

Antonio senior came walking briskly down from the mansion, with Gilimon behind, rubbing his hands. They had agreed on a price, and it was a very good one.

"So that is settled," said Antonio. "At four tomorrow morning I will have the young cattle corralled near the cow sheds. Then we can start loading around five or half past five, if all goes well." Suddenly he caught sight of his son. "What are you standing around for?" he asked. "Have you nothing better to do?"

"It's because of Menardo," Tonio quickly answered. "He is never going to open his mouth again. He has breathed his last."

"Ave María, Alma Bendita," Antonio murmured. "No shortage of problems, that's for sure. Who is going to pray for the cattle now when they have worms, I wonder." He shook his head sadly. "Menardo dead, may God have mercy on his soul, Alma Bendita. . . ."

Tonio nudged Pulga. "Are you coming along to have a look?" he whispered.

But his father said, "Get going Tonio. Pick up a couple of chopping knives. I want you to cut bamboo to go in the truck between the cows. That boy there will lend you a hand. Make sure the pieces you cut are long enough, and look out for snakes—they like bamboo groves. And don't waste time."

When Tonio and Pulga came back with their cut bamboo, it was almost dark. The yard was deserted, but in back of Menardo's cottage a crowd of people had gathered, for the news had spread like a prairie fire. The hacienda farmhands with their families, farmers in the area, with friends and relatives, were sitting in the backyard, where Menardo was laid out on the table in the light of flickering candles. Pulga looked at the emaciated little man, his bony hands folded over his chest, his gray skin in loose folds. Just like a lizard, as Tonio had said.

The women, kneeling around the table, were murmuring prayers. The men stood about in small groups. Bottles of beer and *aguardiente* and gourds of *guarapo*, sugarcane juice, were passed around. Large chunks of meat roasted over an open fire. Everything had been arranged as it should be. One could see that Menardo had been a man of repute.

Who is now going to pray for the cows? the men were wondering.

Who will we call now when a child is sick? the women worried.

What will happen when the birds swarm down over the rice fields, when the rain fails to come and the crops are killed by a drought?

Ave María, what a state of affairs.

"And he knew very well what was going to happen," someone said solemnly. "Last time I talked to him he told me, 'The Indian corn is coming along very well this year, and so is the cotton and the rice . . . they won't need Menardo anymore.' That is what he said, and that is how it is. The crop is firstrate this year, and Menardo knew that he had served his time. Alma Bendita!" And the bottle was passed around once again.

The candles flickered in the night wind. The fire died down. Yet the men and women stayed on. They stayed for the sake of Menardo, who had always prayed for their cattle and their children and their crops. Slowly the moonlight waned, the racket of the crickets subsided. From time to time the dull sound of lowing cattle or the dry cough of a zebu bull could be heard over the dark countryside. A spot of light hovered above the hills.

"A lost soul," someone murmured.

"Or maybe the Madre Monte."

"Ave María, pity him who walks alone in the dead of night over the hills."

Once again the bottle was passed around. One after another the praying women dozed off. From time to time they were awakened briefly by the loud voices and laughter of the men. Then they would resume their prayers, murmuring monotonously, "Ave María, Mother of God. . . ." No one left. All stayed on into the early morning, when the stars began to fade.

It was a good wake. Everybody was there, even Don Roque, the boss. And Tomasa had spared neither expense nor effort. No one could deny that. One could see that Menardo had been a man held in great esteem.

The brand-new pickup from the slaughterhouse came in the morning to carry him away.

16

LOADING CATTLE

Far away in back of Silencio's cottage a cloud of dust rose over the horizon. The ground rumbled. The wild shouts of the *vaqueros* could not be heard yet, and no cattle were in sight.

Silencio's wife came out of her smoke-filled little kitchen next to the cottage. She carried a cracked cup of steaming black coffee, and behind her came two little girls with gourds that were also filled with coffee.

The cracked cup was for Don Roque. The gourds were for Gilimon and Antonio and Pulga. After his sleepless night, Pulga savored the hot, unsweetened drink better than anything he ever had tasted.

Sitting in one of the hammocks, which Silencio's wife hung especially for the rare occasion of visitors, Pulga enjoyed his coffee sip by sip. It awakened him fully and he looked around at his surroundings with concentrated interest.

The cottage was hardly more than a roof of palm leaves supported by wooden poles. On the clay wall, which was no more than a yard high, he saw several saddles. Lassos, made of braided strips of cowhide, and neatly rolled, hung from big curved horns that were attached to the poles supporting the roof. A sow with piglets was busily grunting and searching on the floor of trampled earth, and near the dark little lean-to a couple of chickens were scratching for worms.

The woman, who had remained standing near Don Roque with her children in order to relieve him of his empty cup, peered into the gray distance. "There they come, boss," she said. She took the empty cup and disappeared with her offspring inside the dark kitchen.

Over the hills came the first animals. Galloping, snorting, and roaring, they stampeded across the hazy land toward the *vaquería*. Swarthy men on spirited little horses surrounded the herd, their loud, shrill voices resounding in the morning air.

Loading Cattle

The first animals, the *madrina*, which had been trained to lead, raced into the corral. The wild herd of younger cattle followed blindly. They galloped alongside the heavy wooden fence, their powerful heads with sweeping horns battering against the stockade. Some of the animals tried to force their way out through the heavy planks, roaring, stampeding, but in the end they calmed down, pressed together in one corner of the corral.

Slowly Don Roque got up from his hammock. Antonio and Gilimon followed, with Pulga in the rear. Silencio and the other *vaqueros* dismounted, exchanged greetings, and walked toward the corral. For a while they watched the restless, milling animals. Then they entered the corral, directly in the center of the nervous cattle. The heavy, beamed gate was closed after them. Gilimon and Pulga stayed outside, and Pulga climbed up on the stockade.

When Don Roque, together with his foreman and the *vaqueros*, went inside the corral, the animals became still more restive. They bent down and shook their small heads with their pointed horns. Some seemed poised for attack, while others withdrew to the farthest corner of the corral, instinctively joining the herd to which they belonged. The younger animals stood in small groups around the leaders. They snorted, lowed, and pawed the ground, while the *vaqueros* walked about, whirling their lassos.

Don Roque pointed to various animals. "That one there . . . and that one . . . and the little gray one with the dark spots."

The *vaqueros* mingled with the cattle; their raised lassos began to turn faster. Close to the stockade the animals began to run around again. They pushed against each other, their horns got entangled and came loose, they jumped over each other. With horns and hooves they tore one another's hide. Wildly they kept galloping around and around the corral.

The dust blew high, and higher up swung the lassos, the ends scarcely moving in the hands of the *vaqueros*. Then they were let go, circling over the packed horde of madly racing cattle. One lasso fell on the neck of the gray heifer with dark spots and slid off. Another was slung over her head and pulled tightly around her neck. Maddened with fright, she kept running. Other *vaqueros* came over and hung onto the end of the lasso.

Gradually the herd slowed down. The animals seemed to sense that for the moment the danger was over. Again they gathered in one corner of the corral, snorting, roaring, and stamping.

The little gray cow, the lasso tight around her neck, made a last desperate attempt to get away. Then she calmed down, breathless, her head lowered, nostrils wide open. One of the *vaqueros* quickly

Loading Cattle

grabbed the animal's tail and gave it a smart quarter turn. With a thud she fell to the ground and lay there, her neck stretched out, eyes bulging, nostrils distended. Another *vaquero* stood up on the animal's flank and pulled her tail forward between the hind legs. Silencio walked over leisurely, placed his dirty bare foot on top of the animal's head, and dug his big toe into the eye socket.

The cow lay still, breathing heavily. One of the men came over with the *cequeta*, a small saw with very fine teeth. The sharp tips of the horns were sawed off. Blood dripped on the ground, and creosote was brushed over the bleeding horns. Then the men jumped back, the lasso was payed out, and the little gray cow jumped up like a bolt of lightning and galloped, snorting, head swaying, back to the herd.

Again the *vaqueros* moved in, mingling with the cattle. Again the lassos were swung around and around, and again the cattle started their wild race, snorting, stamping, roaring. Dust rose high into the air, the lassos were flung out and fell down over the horns of the animals that Don Roque had pointed out. Their bodies fell with heavy thuds to the ground, their tails were twisted between their hind feet, the dirty toe of Silencio dug into their eye sockets. Blood flowed under the sharp teeth of the little saw. The quiet of the early morning hour was torn by the laughter and shouting of the *vaqueros* and the dull roar of the cattle.

Finally Don Roque came up to the gate. "We are ready to begin loading," he said to Gilimon. "Back up your truck against the ramp."

The ten animals to be shipped were driven with sticks through the narrow passage, up the concrete ramp, and into the truck. Sliding, resisting, they moved slowly to their assigned places, where they were fastened between the bamboo partitions. The tail gate was closed. The closely packed cattle stood pawing the straw that had been spread over the floor, knocking their heads and bleeding horns against the wooden frame of the truck. The heavy vehicle vibrated under the impact.

"Let's go!" Don Roque ordered.

Gilimon was already behind the wheel. Pulga was about to jump into the cab when Gilimon motioned him back. "There's no room for you in front, Pulga. Two of the boys from the hacienda are coming along to Copacabana."

"No room . . . but . . . but where can I . . . ?" he stammered.

"Back there with the cattle."

"Back there with the . . . with those beasts? They are going to. . . ." Before Pulga could say another word, one of the *vaqueros* lifted him off the ground and swung him high up on the tail gate.

"Give the boy a stick so he has something to hit back with when things get out of hand," Silencio ordered.

Someone handed Pulga a stick. He heard the doors of the cab slam shut. Slowly the truck began moving. Jolting and bumping, they rolled off with their living freight, following the narrow path up and around and over the hills. They drove across the yard of the hacienda, past the white mansion, past Menardo's cabin. Everything was quiet there. The door stood ajar. Chickens were scratching under the table where Menardo had been laid out.

They drove through the gate of Las Palmas and turned onto the long road that led to Copacabana, through the green countryside, along the Cauca River, up into the mountains. Slowly the truck made the steep incline. The motor throbbed. Black clouds of stinking smoke trailed behind.

Perched on the tail gate, Pulga held on with all his strength and looked down at the restless animals. Deprived of their freedom, they lowed nervously as though begrudging their companions their share of space. Their heavy, perspiring bodies rubbed against each other. The heads with long curved horns battered the wooden siding. Hooves scraped away the straw and trampled the wood underneath. The whole body of the truck creaked and trembled.

Pulga kept staring at the restless, moving bodies

below, within easy reach of his feet. Sweat trickled down his face and neck, but he did not dare wipe it off. With both hands he held onto the slats of the gate, digging his fingernails into the wood. He had long since lost his stick. It had dropped down and was trampled by the numberless feet. What if he were to fall down there? Ave María . . . the very thought made his stomach turn.

They stopped for a breakfast of meat and *arepas* and a cup of chocolate. Later in the day they had big plates of brown beans and yucca, with *panela* water to quench their thirst. For the first time in his life Pulga ate slowly. He had intended to ask how far they still had to go, but Gilimon and the two men from Las Palmas were busy talking and paid no attention to him. Scared stiff, he climbed clumsily back on top of the tail gate.

They drove on and on, up into the mountains. Crowded buses, their horns blowing, dashed past on the narrow road. Clouds of dust whirled up.

Beyond Yarumal the weather suddenly changed. Dark clouds rose over the mountains, drifting toward them, and then rain came pouring down from the leaden sky. It flowed down the mountain slopes, filling crevices and ravines, hitting the road in foaming waterfalls.

Across a torrent of water, the heavy truck slid into one of the numerous deep ruts. Some of the

Loading Cattle

animals lost their balance and tumbled over, flailing their legs wildy against the body of the truck. The bamboo poles were crushed to splinters. The side panels shook. Foaming water splashed over the hood, the cab, the tail gate.

Pulga no longer saw anything. The gray of the cattle and of the water merged before his eyes. Instinctively he moved one of his hands and lost his balance. With a muffled scream he slid down.

His fingers clutched the top board of the tail gate. Kicking desperately, he hung on inside the truck. Water got into his nose, his ears, his mouth. He was being dragged down by the water, down among the wet, steaming bodies of the cattle . . . drowning. . . .

He gasped for air. Drowning, apparently, was not as good a death as the driver in Fundación had claimed it to be. . . .

For a second he felt as though he were pressed into a niche of warm clothing. Where had he gone through something like that? Oh yes, in Bogotá when he opened the front door. . . . The picture faded as the water poured down over him, bringing another memory: a delapidated building, a dripping rain pipe, a flooded patio. The house where he used to live. . . .

So this was the way someone felt when the end was near, when he went down in rushing water and billowing bodies. This was the way the helper must have felt when he drowned near the ferry across the Magdalena River . . . and Fermin, when he walked through the wet grass toward the dark edge of the woods. One against three. . . . Who had said that? The old woman Obdulia! One against three . . . ten against one. . . . So that was it! In a flash a person's entire life passed before him.

What sort of life? What had it been?

A dingy room where he had lived with his grandmother and his sisters. And Pedro. Pedro and he had been together most of the time, and yet Pulga had not even told him that he was going away with Gilimon. And then the short stay with Mamá Maruja in the sun-bathed little valley . . . the attack of highwaymen, when he was lying motionless on the axle with Gilimon's suitcase and heard the footsteps of the bandits around the truck. But he had not really lived through all that with full awareness. Not the way he was now. . . . "Ave María, Virgen Santa, have mercy upon me. . . ."

Again the truck swayed, the pressure of the cows' bodies shifted, the worst was over. Pulga could breathe again. The rain kept coming down in torrents, but he could breathe again.

His left foot found support on the bony hindquarter of one of the animals. He worked himself up, the feat taking great effort, but he managed. A

Loading Cattle

young zebu steer, his horns caught between the boards of the tail gate, jerked and twisted his head wildly. The tendons in his neck stretched to the breaking point as he struggled to back out. He pulled and pushed and roared, striking out in all directions. His horns cracked and broke off.

The sidings of the truck shook and creaked. Pulga hung by his arms, clinging desperately to the top crossbar of the tail gate, trying with his bare toes to get a hold in the cracks between the boards. Slowly he worked himself up farther. He was sitting again. . . . He had no feeling in his back, his arms, his legs, his buttocks, but he was sitting again.

The zebu steer now stood stock-still, panting heavily, his gory head bent down. From deep inside him came a shuddering, coughlike moan.

One of the men in front stuck his head out through the cab window. "Everything all right back there?" he shouted.

Pulga did not answer as he stared at the series of small wooden crosses, standing crooked and by now quite unaligned, beyond the precipice near Mata Sano. It suddenly dawned on him how many wooden crosses lined this road. Perhaps if he counted them, time would pass faster. But he quickly gave up. Dazed and numb, wet through and chilled, he sat there waiting for them to reach their destination.

The rain stopped as suddenly as it had begun.

When they turned into a side road outside of Copacabana and drove up to the yard of the Hacienda Aguadulce, it was dry. Before the truck had stopped fully, Pulga slid down to the ground. His knees were wobbly, his legs trembled, and his fingers refused to uncurl. Stiffly he rubbed his hands together and cautiously straightened his back.

Gilimon stopped the motor, and the three men climbed out and walked up the yard.

Pulga heard the high chirping of crickets and the eerie squeaking of sugarcane mills. In the soft light of dusk he could make out the shape of the oxen that kept the mills going. They walked slowly and heavily, around and around, in the same circle. A man drove them on, while a woman in a straw hat fed the long canes with monotonous regularity between the grinding stones. The sweet smell of the dark sap mingled with the scent of flowers and wet soil.

Pulga picked up a piece of sugarcane that was lying on the ground. It tasted sweet and juicy, and made him feel more like himself again.

The manager and the foreman of the hacienda came running.

"Is that the cattle from Las Palmas?" the manager asked Gilimon. "What a quick delivery. I did not think they could arrive today."

After the cattle were driven off the truck into a

corral, Gilimon examined his truck. It was quite a sight and it reeked of blood and manure. Gilimon looked around for his helper.

"Pulga, what's the idea?" he called out. "Standing around as though you had nothing to do but chew sugarcane. Get busy! The whole truck stinks! Spruce it up a little. You haven't done anything but warm your behind!"

17

THE STORYTELLERS

The little shop of Jesús and Carmenza was a busy place. Groups of men sat drinking beer and *aguardiente* on the moonlit grounds around it. Women lingered after completing the day's shopping: a bag of barley meal, a box of matches, a candle, three cigarettes, a piece of *panela*. They stayed to talk over the day's news, to gossip, to listen.

Through the darkness that had settled over the land, under the starry sky, they came up from the valley and down from the sloping hillsides. The men wore cotton *ruanas*, and the *peinilla*, a long, narrow chopping knife, dangled from their hips. The faces of the women, whose long black braids hung over their bent backs, were almost hidden under straw hats. Noiselessly they walked along the paths, which years of use had engraved on the countryside, to the small, whitewashed house where Jesús skillfully opened one bottle of beer after another while Carmenza squatted against the wall, mashing Indian corn.

The eerie squeaking of the sugarcane mills was no longer heard. Only the shrill chirping of crickets and the low call of frogs pierced the stillness of the night. The wind rustled through the crowns of the palm trees.

Gilimon, with a glass of beer in his hand, was standing with a group of men near the door of the store, where Jesús was busy behind the grimy counter.

A little farther along, though still close enough not to miss a word, Pulga was sweeping the last reminders of their recent freight off the truck. He must never again give Gilimon a chance to tell him that he was shirking his duties, especially now when they were so close to the last leg of their journey!

He spat on the windshield and vigorously polished it with his frayed, red rag. His belly was full of brown beans, and he felt more like himself again. Meanwhile, he kept his ears wide open.

Down at Don Pablo's they had a relatively good crop—it could have been much worse. But farther along at Las Mercedes the rain of the last few weeks had done much damage. And this side of Sonsón the road was closed. Yes, a landslide. To get through a man had to be a goat. All the freight for La Dorada now had to go by way of Manizales. Some fun for the drivers! These days no one could be sure of the weather. After all, this was December, and the dry season should have begun by now.

At Aunt Margarita's all the chickens had caught coryza, and Don Jaime had a couple of sick cows. Keep your fingers crossed, lest it be hoof-and-mouth disease! Imagine, just when the cows from Las Palmas had arrived at Aguadulce.

In the mountains of Caldas and Tolima bandits had had a field day once again. One settlement had been burned to the ground, the bandits had raided a *finca*, and at one of the large plantations the owner had been kidnapped as a hostage. Yes, there was good reason to think that it was the work of Sombra Negra and his gang. Sombra Negra was smooth as an eel, impossible to get hold of. Like a black shadow, he went gliding through the mountains, through the night. . . .

"*Maldito sea* . . . cursed be his soul. . . ."

"Your life is no longer safe anywhere. Ave María!"

"Indeed, there is no shortage of problems."

"You can say that again."

The night wind blew through the treetops, and the dark feathery fronds of the palms swayed to and fro. A star fell beyond the hills over the horizon.

"Virgen Santa," mumbled Carmenza, "if that does not mean someone is dying tonight. . . ." She hastily made the sign of the Cross.

"And I wouldn't be surprised if someone did," said one of the men.

At Las Mercedes two men had been quarreling. About a girl of course. The duel might take place this night.

Hush . . . one should not talk about such things.

These fights in which two men fought each other with their *peinillas* till one of them was mortally wounded had long since been forbidden, and it was wise not to speak about them. There would be excitement enough when the time came.

"Jaime's woman has come back from the coast with the whole brood. I saw her myself at El Piñal."

"You must be joking."

"It's the honest-to-goodness truth."

"I still can't believe it."

"She did not want to stay there. Jaime himself felt differently about it. He had a good job and a good boss. But that woman of his was seeing ghosts. The ghost of the son of the previous owner, who had been murdered and who was looking for his hand...."

"Ai ... ai ... what a life!"

Pulga threw his red rag inside the cab and walked a few steps closer to the group. He did not want to miss any of the conversation. Jaime and his woman and her brood were, of course, the people they had picked up just outside Cartagena, who had tried to sneak off at Sincelejo with two bags of their cement. He cast a knowing glance at Gilimon, but Gilimon said nothing and the talk continued.

"And what has happened to that little fellow, Torbilio?"

"Torbilio! Don't you know?"

"He should not have gone is my opinion."

"At night in the hills it is dangerous."

"He went out to cut *fique* for his father, late at night under a new moon. He did not come back. No one has seen him. Alma Bendita!"

"The Patasola?"

"Yes, the Patasola or La Candileja or the Madre Monte ... no one knows. One of the souls in torment that roam through the mountains, haunting the hills."

The Patasola moving about on one leg. The Candileja, a small flickering light that pursues lost wanderers along deserted paths. And the Madre Monte, calling children in the dark of night, in rain and foul weather, taking them with her, God knows where to! Into the ravines of the mountains, under the lush, green fern leaves, or among the boulders along the riverbanks.

"Poor little Torbilio . . . may God have mercy upon his soul!"

The wind was stronger now. Pulga could hear the rustling of the trees, the swaying of the palms. One after another the stars were lost from sight. The moon disappeared behind a heavy cover of clouds. It began to rain, big lukewarm drops. The men and women got ready to go home, to their little cottages down in the village or higher up along the sloping hills. Walking in groups, they disappeared along the narrow paths into the darkness.

Pulga climbed into the cab. He felt safe there. Not for anything in the world would he go out now into the darkness and over the hills. Just imagine, a small, yellow flicker of a flame suddenly dancing along your path, ahead of you, behind you, pursuing you to the end of time. And the Madre Monte! Could a person hear her? Could he see her? Or was it simply that he felt the black woolen cover glide over him? A shiver crept down Pulga's spine.

Did little Torbilio know what was happening to him, the poor fellow who had gone out to cut *fique* leaves for his father? Surely, his father had taught him how to use the razor-sharp chopping knife.

Surely his father had taught him how to defend himself with the *peinilla*. But there was nothing anyone could do when the Madre Monte came. . . .

Pulga shivered again, and was glad when Gilimon joined him. They wrapped themselves up in their *ruanas*.

"There we are," Gilimon said. "Tomorrow morning we drive into Medellín and pick up some freight for Bogotá. And that will be that. Another round trip in the bag." Pulga could tell from his voice how pleased Gilimon was.

Bogotá! Pulga's heart sank. This then was the last leg of their trip. Suddenly Bogotá was no longer far away. The big, musty-smelling house loomed up before him. He could see the dark hole in the wall where he lived with his grandmother and his sisters and with Pedro. He could feel the cold of the cobbled passageway; he could smell the garbage. At the end of the trip he would have to live once again in the old house, he would have to roam the streets in search of something to eat. That is what lay ahead of him.

Or possibly Gilimon would ask him to stay on, to go with him again as his helper. . . . He hardly dared think of such a possibility. Should he try. . . ? He had been doing his very best . . . would it be too much if he. . . ? Stealthily he looked at Gilimon.

"Yes," said Gilimon, "out with it."

"When we are in Bogotá . . ." Pulga began, but then suddenly he did not have the courage to ask the question on his mind. What if Gilimon were to turn him down? Then he would have nothing left . . . no hope . . . no future . . . nothing to look forward to.

"I mean," he said instead, "when are we going to be in Bogotá? Tomorrow?"

"Tomorrow," mumbled Gilimon. "Are you in such a hurry to get home? It's still a small matter of six hundred kilometers through the mountains! If I can swing it, I want to get through the bandit area before nightfall."

Through the bandit area! Through the area where Sombra Negra ruled, destroying and killing. Ave María, how could he have forgotten about that? Pulga passed his tongue over his dry lips.

Gilimon went on, following his own thoughts. "The road from Medillín through the Valle de Risaralda is fine, and that far we'll have no trouble. Then come the mountains, the central chain of the Andes into the valley of the Magdalena River. And then, on the other side of the river, we start all over again, going up and up to Bogotá. Day after tomorrow we'll be home, if things work out halfway." Gilimon heaved a deep sigh. "Ave María, what a life!" He had just about had it.

Pulga sighed too, a sigh of relief. For the time

being he had nothing to worry about. Two whole days were still ahead of him, two days with something to eat three times each day. And there was a good chance that Gilimon might say something to him during that time. He might ask Pulga, in a casual sort of way, to go with him on his next journey as his helper. And in Bogotá he was to get his money, his first earned wages. Right away he would buy a pair of shoes—that was certain—and then something for his grandmother and his sisters and Pedro. What a surprise they would have when he came home with all those beautiful things! And Pedro—he would want to tell Pedro all about his adventures.

In any event, they could not travel at night through the mountains of Caldas into Tolima, those forsaken mountains haunted by the Madre Monte and infested by bandits. Things seemed to look a little brighter. There were still two whole days without anything to worry about.

Luckily, Pulga did not have the gift of the old woman Obdulia; luckily he could not look into the future.

18

THE TRUNK OF THE DEVIL
Copacabana to Bogotá

Next morning when Gilimon came out of the shipping office in Madellín, he looked anything but pleased. While climbing into the truck, he said, "OK then, let's go pick up the freight for Manizales they have for us at the textile factory."

"Manizales?" said Pulga. "I thought we were going—"

"So did I. Well, there you have it. In our business you never can tell what's coming up next. As far as I'm concerned, it would have been nice if they had sent us on all the way to Bogotá. Oh, well, it's not so very far out of our way. In Manizales we should have no trouble finding something for the last leg of the trip. Tomorrow night we ought to be in Bogotá, if things work out decently."

But things didn't.

The road through the Valle de Risaralda was crowded with cars and trucks that could not go by way of Sonsón, where the landslide had not yet been removed. They also had motor trouble. When they arrived in Manizales in the early afternoon, they delivered their cargo and then took the truck to a repair shop to have it looked over. And that, said the mechanic, could not be done before the next day. They should come back to check sometime around noon.

"As long as you remember that I have to get to Bogotá before tomorrow night," said Gilimon emphatically.

The mechanic shrugged his shoulders. "All right," he said without the slightest concern, "around noontime. We'll be ready for you then."

Next morning Gilimon spent his time running around from one freight office to another. When he finally came back with a fistful of bills of lading, his face looked like a storm cloud.

"It couldn't be worse," he said to Pulga, who had stayed with the truck to observe what the mechanics were doing to the motor. "We have refrigerators

The Trunk of the Devil

for Mariquita and Armero and Espinal and Girardot, all the little hot places in the Magdalena valley. The milk run to Bogotá! It's as though the Devil had a hand in it."

Pulga had little to say. As far as he was concerned, nothing could be too slow. Three meals a day was something he had never experienced before this trip with Gilimon. And it was quite clear to him that he no longer could take them for granted once he was back in Bogotá.

Of course, the truck was not ready at twelve o'clock. Two hours later they left the repair shop, picked up the refrigerators, and sometime in the afternoon they finally left Manizales.

The road took them almost immediately into the mountains. Manizales dropped out of sight behind them in the green hill country of palms and banana trees and patches of bamboo.

The mountains rose tall and bluish, their steep peaks hidden behind clouds. The gray snowcaps of Monte Ruiz and Monte Santa Isabel disappeared in the fog. They had reached the high mountain wasteland with its gullies and ravines, its sheer rock walls and dizzying precipices, the central chain of the Andes.

After some time Gilimon said, "We've had no oncoming traffic since God knows when. I'm beginning to wonder."

"I also noticed that," Pulga said. Actually he had not paid much attention to the oncoming traffic, but now that Gilimon had mentioned it, he, too, was struck by its absence.

They drove on in silence over the deserted road winding up into the mountains. Just after passing one of the many bends, Gilimon slammed on the brakes. Lined up ahead of them stood a row of cars. People were standing around, busily talking and gesticulating, or walking back and forth.

Gilimon and Pulga went over to investigate. Farther up a bulldozer was clearing the road where a mass of muddy soil and rocks and bushes had been dumped by a landslide.

"The first thing that came to mind was, it's a holdup," said a woman, carrying an infant who seemed to be overcome by the heat in her arms.

"I've been told that Sombra Negra and his gang are somewhere around here."

"Ave María, that tops it!"

Gilimon walked up to a driver who was sitting quietly in his pickup, reading a newspaper. "How long is this going to last?" he asked, not hiding his annoyance.

"Why ask me?" answered the man. "They're working on it."

"Imagine if they weren't!" Gilimon growled. "This is no place to spend the night."

The driver raised an eyebrow. "I wouldn't say that too loud," he replied laconically. "It may still turn out that way."

Gilimon shrugged his shoulders. He was thoroughly exasperated. The man produced a bottle of *aguardiente* from his pocket.

"Come on, brother, have one on me," he said calmly. "You never can tell, this may be our last." They took turns drinking.

The mountaintops all around were wrapped in a bluish haze of rain. The road was hot, the sun stinging. The broad steel blade of the bulldozer scraped over the road, shoving rocks, soil, and broken tree trunks over the side into the valley below. By now the road was cleared enough for passage, and the vehicles began to move slowly. One after another they bumped along in the scorching sun, over potholes and through mud puddles.

For a while the vehicles kept in line as they drove over the winding road through the mountains. Then the lighter cars pulled ahead of the heavily laden trucks. Soon everyone had passed out of sight, and Gilimon and Pulga once again had the road to themselves.

A thin fog began to rise, the vegetation became sparse, and now it was biting cold. They were on the Páramo de Letras. A vivid, yellow light hung over the plateau. The creeping bushes and stiff foliage seemed to breathe. A keen, icy wind blew down from the snowcapped mountains.

Through the patches of fog they could see the outlines of several wretched huts along the road. Gilimon stopped the truck and began blowing on his hands. "Let's have a look, Pulga. Maybe they have something warm for us."

With their *ruanas* tightly wrapped around their shoulders, they climbed out of the cab and walked across to one of the huts. Outside the door, on a shaky table, stood a pot full of sweet potatoes and a few bottles of beer and *aguardiente*. They continued on into the smoke-filled shack where a woman was busy cooking over a charcoal fire between two large slabs of stone. Two shivering children and a man with a toothless, sunken mouth and a big drop of mucus hanging at the tip of his nose sat huddled on the warm slabs around the fire.

The woman picked a couple of sweet potatoes from a pot on the table, dropped them on the plate in front of Pulga, and shoved a glass of *aguardiente* toward Gilimon.

"That should help against the cold," Gilimon said. He downed the drink on one swallow and pushed the empty glass back across the table.

Pulga, chewing on a cold, half-cooked potato, stepped over to stand closer by the fire.

"Heading toward Manizales?" asked the man.

"Heading toward Bogotá," Pulga answered.

"I see, Bogotá," said the man in a peculiar drawl, and nodded thoughtfully. The drop at the tip of his nose grew longer and fell into the pot on the fire. "That is quite a stretch yet."

"It is," Pulga confirmed. He stared outside through the window. Wet grayish clouds were rolling over the road. "Is it still a long distance through the mountains?" he asked.

"A long distance through the mountains. . . ." the man repeated. "My poor fellow, you've hardly begun!" He sucked his lower lip, and his nose seemed to stick out still farther. "You had better watch out when you pass the Trompa del Diablo," he said slowly.

"Pass what?" Pulga asked, fear in his wide-open eyes.

"The Trunk of the Devil. Out there, farther up. . . . You wouldn't be the first to get caught there for good."

"But . . . but what is it?" Pulga asked, his voice slightly hoarse.

"Oh, rocks—nothing but vertical walls of rock—where the Devil's Trunk wriggles around."

Pulga stared outside again. The icy wind had begun to drive the clouds away, high above the precipices and across the mountain crests. The road was visible again.

"A good thing it's clearing a little," he said. To himself he thought, If we get past those rocks by daylight, the Devil won't be able to get us. He was hoping that Gilimon would hurry a little, but his boss was having another *aguardiente*. The woman took the pot off the fire and set it on the table next to the other. Later on some more hungry and shivering travelers would arrive.

The man on the warm slab bent forward a little. The glow of the fire played over his furrowed face; spittle ran slowly from his mouth. As though he had read Pulga's thoughts, he said, "You don't think that once you get past those rocks, you'll have nothing further to worry about, do you? If I were you, I wouldn't count on it." He grinned cagily. "The Devil's Trunk reaches far, over all the mountainsides, over the ridges, deep down into the valley. You would not be the first to be hauled in at the last minute." He grinned again and sucked his lower lip still farther inward. His withered face and sharp nose glowed in the firelight.

That one could be the Devil himself, Pulga thought, and shuddered. He was glad when Gilimon finally put his empty glass on the table, paid their bill, and motioned Pulga to come along. Without a word or a gesture of good-bye, he left the smoke-filled shack. From behind Pulga heard the man's uncanny laughter.

The road ahead was swept clean by the wind, and before them rose a dark, fantastically shaped mountain, drawing closer and closer. Along its side the road looked like a whimsical pencil line.

Here . . . this is it, Pulga thought. He clutched the frame of the windshield.

Between the vertical rock wall on the one side and the gaping abyss on the other, the road appeared to be growing narrower. The heavy truck seemed hardly more than a tiny ant . . . a moving dot in the majestic grandeur of the massif.

"Why do you sit there looking glum?" said Gilimon, obviously amused by Pulga's fidgeting.

Pulga no longer tried to look brave. "Is this . . . is this the Devil's Trunk?" he asked meekly.

"Yes, we've almost reached the end of it. Over there, around the bend where the rock sticks out, we'll begin to go downhill."

Gilimon was right. Gradually the road did begin to slant downhill, but the walls of rock remained steep and forbidding, and the abyss was still unfathomably deep. Ahead of them another range of mountains rose up, endless mountain chains as far as the eye could see.

Darkness fell. All the colors vanished, and all light was drawn from the earth. Out of the ravines and the gorges, darkness settled down in purple patches along the mountainsides and mingled with the dusk that formed in the depths of the valleys.

The road was deserted. The doors and windows of cottages that were scattered along the way were closed. Not a soul was to be seen anywhere. This was the bandit area.

Slowly a fine drizzle fell. The yellow headlights of the truck swept over the road. The windshield wipers kept ticking rhythmically. Though it had become warmer inside the cab, Pulga remained huddled up in his corner, his *ruana* wrapped tightly around his shoulders.

"Near Delgadita we're going to cross the ridge," said Gilimon. "That's the way we got into Tolima."

The rain stopped, and the moon rose round and full over the mountains of Tolima. The steep slopes of the Caldas massif were driven back into the night.

Pulga sat up and slipped out of his *ruana*. He heaved a sigh of relief. Here, he thought, here we are out of reach of the Devil's Trunk.

At that moment the truck slipped. Gilimon threw all his strength into the steering wheel. But the front of the truck was in a ditch, and the running board and the side of the cab scratched along the uneven rock wall, shooting off sparks. The truck limped on for a few feet, then came to a halt, resting against the cliff.

Cursing and swearing, Gilimon stepped out. "Here we are," he said.

"Yes," said Pulga.

"A narrow escape," said Gilimon.

Then they both fell silent. In the vast stillness they heard the rushing waters of a river far below in the valley.

Gilimon examined the truck carefully from front to rear. "The running board and the cab door got the worst of it, and the canvas all along this side is badly torn." He looked at the wheels that had slipped into the ditch. "They don't look too good either."

Pulga could not speak. He just stood there trying to stop his legs from shaking. What he would have liked best was to sit down, anywhere, even in the middle of the road, but he did not dare.

Gilimon picked up a rock and wedged it under the front wheel that was still on the road.

"Go on, Pulga, find a couple of rocks like this one for the rear wheels and set up the red triangles. You ought to know about all that by now."

Pulga bit his lips. Why hadn't he thought of doing so by himself? Quickly he got busy, trying to make up for his oversight.

Again they fell silent. The moon cast its light over the landscape. Water trickled down from the fern fronds and the low bushes along the ditch. Crickets were chirping, and fireflies flickered in the underbrush.

Finally Gilimon said, "Something has to be done. You'll have to go and get help."

"Me?" Pulga asked.

"Yes, you. Who else?"

Pulga swallowed. "Where . . . who to . . . where do you want me to go?"

"To some hacienda or a village or something along the river. There are always people living there. You'll see. . . ." Gilimon turned around, walked over to the tilted truck, climbed into the cab, and stretched out his legs in the most comfortable position possible. "And make it fast!" he called out. "I don't feel like camping here all night."

For a moment Pulga stood there, glued to the road. Then he quickly stepped into the long grass between the ferns and the rotting piles of foliage. Groping his way, he started down the hillside into the valley.

When he looked back, the truck and Gilimon were out of sight.

19

THE HACIENDA LA VIRGINIA

At La Virginia all the lights were on. Over the railing of the broad veranda one could look out far into the garden. The *copas de oro* were glistening like pure gold, and the red and purple bougainvillas were swaying gently in the night wind. The soft, yellowish light from the house reached as far as the high poinsettia bushes, whose top leaves shone blood red. Between the poinsettias one could see the still water of the swimming pool and the edge of the great coffee groves just beyond. The coffee bushes were lying in darkness under the high shade trees.

Here and there the moonlight filtered through the branches, exposing the dark, glossy green leaves of the coffee plants.

In the large living room, the doors of which led onto the veranda, Don Gabriel was sitting at his desk poring over his account books. A servant girl entered noiselessly with a large glass of lemonade on a small tray.

Don Gabriel did not look up, but his son, Jorge Gabriel, who was sitting on the veranda busily repairing his horse's bridle, called out, "Let me have a glass of lemonade, too, Belén!"

"Me, too! One for me, too!" Ana María cried in her shrill voice.

Her older sister, Beatriz, nudged her with her elbow. "Be quiet, otherwise Mother will hear us and then she'll send us to bed."

"But I'm thirsty," Ana María objected.

"Nonsense," said Beatriz firmly. She pulled her little sister along with her to the farthest corner of the veranda, where all their dolls were lying on lawn chairs and in hammocks, which, by some magic, had turned into beds.

"I'm going to wash my dolls before they go to bed," said Beatriz. "That's what Mother does to us. And I'm going to wash their hair too."

"Me, too," Ana María cried delightedly. She

already had forgotten about the lemonade. "I'm going to wash my dolls' hair too. I'm going to wash this one's hair first." She held up her biggest, most beautiful doll, the one with blond curls and a tulle dress.

Jorge Gabriel looked up from his work. "You shouldn't do that, Ana María. You just got that doll. You're going to mess her all up!"

"Who cares?" said Ana María, without the slightest respect for her big brother. She exchanged a conniving glance with her sister. "I'm going to wash her hair, and I'm going to give her a real bath. That's the way it must be done," she said in a lower voice so that their brother could not hear her. But Jorge Gabriel already had gone back to fixing his bridle, putting in new side straps and trying to shorten the crosspiece.

"Where are we going to get the water?" Beatriz asked.

"Oh, I'll get that in the kitchen," Ana María suggested.

"From the kitchen? Are you that dumb? If you do, Belén will see you, and then she tells Mother, and then we have to go to bed right away. No, we have to think of something better." Deep in thought, she looked around, and then her face lit up. "I know . . . from the pool. You run down to the swimming pool and come back with all the water you want."

"The swimming pool. . . ." Ana María said hesitatingly. She looked out over the wide lawn and the flowers glistening in the light from the house. Beyond lay the garden in almost complete darkness. Farther down, at the swimming pool, it certainly was still darker. Bathing the dolls suddenly seemed less attractive.

"Are there frogs in the garden?" asked Ana María.

"Of course not, what makes you think that?"

"When it's been raining, there are always frogs around. Those big ones."

Light footsteps could be heard coming from the garden. A man stepped out of the shadows into the circle of light. He walked slowly up to the big house and stopped at the steps leading up to the veranda.

Jorge Gabriel looked up. "Good evening, Alejandro," he said to the foreman.

"Good evening, *señor*. Is your father Don Gabriel around?"

"He's inside, in the living room."

"May I?"

"Go right in."

Alejandro walked silently across the veranda,

stopped hat in hand at the door leading inside, and cleared his throat to make his presence known.

Don Gabriel looked up. "Alejandro, what have you to report?"

"Nothing in particular, *señor*."

"Did you get down to the coffee groves today?"

"Yes, sir."

"And so?"

"The coffee is coming along nicely, *señor*. The pickers are busy. We can't complain about the crop."

"That was my impression. You were down at the Small Plain, too, weren't you?"

"No, *señor*."

Don Gabriel raised his eyebrows. "How so?"

"*Pues*, I did not get there."

"I thought you were to go out there today to have a look at the cattle."

Don Gabriel waited silently.

Finally Alejandro explained. "You see, *señor*, the thing is, our little boy has been sick for quite a while. He coughs and keeps on coughing."

"Is that so? I didn't know about it."

"No, *señor*. I went over to the village several times to get medicine. But medicine is expensive, and it doesn't help."

"Why didn't you go to see Doña Dora right away? You know that my wife. . . ."

"Yes, *señor*, but I didn't want to bother Doña Dora unless it was really necessary. And then someone told me I should cut off the beard of a goat and make an extract of it in warm milk to give the boy to drink. So I went looking this afternoon, but they asked ten pesos, just for the beard—without the goat."

"There you are. You had better go straight to Doña Dora and ask her whether she has a remedy for your little boy. You'll go tomorrow morning to look at the cattle."

"Yes, *señor*, I'll do that tomorrow morning."

"So that is settled," said Don Gabriel, nodding, and he went back to his bookkeeping chores.

But Alejandro did not leave. He cleared his throat once again and said, "This afternoon two men walked through the coffee groves up there."

Impatiently Don Gabriel looked up. "Two men," he repeated rather curtly.

"Yes, *señor*."

"What sort of men? What do you mean?"

"There were two of them. They walked through the groves."

"What sort of men were they? Any idea?"

"It's hard to say. There were two of them. They walked across the plantation."

"Were they looking for work? They may have come to pick."

The Hacienda La Virginia

"No, *señor*, I don't think so. They just walked across the groves. I never saw them before."

Don Gabriel shrugged impatiently. Alejandro bade him good evening, wished him a good night's rest, and disappeared quietly into the garden.

Beatriz saw him leave and nudged her sister. "There goes Alejandro. Hurry, follow him all the way to the swimming pool. That way you won't be alone in the garden. I'll wait here for you. Hurry now!" She handed Ana María a small plastic pail and gently pushed her ahead. Hesitantly, Ana María walked off into the garden. Alejandro, however, was out of sight. The wind rustled through the tall shade trees of the coffee groves. Along the poinsettia bushes she could see the reflection from the water in the swimming pool. Quickly Ana María walked over to the edge of the pool and bent down to fill her little pail with water.

Jorge Gabriel finally got the bridle repaired and proudly took it inside to show his father. "I've fixed up the bridle for my horse," he said. "I put in new side pieces for the bit, but I'm afraid the throatlatch is short now. I think I'll go and see whether I can find a better one in the tack room."

"Fine, fine," his father said absentmindedly.

"Is Alejandro going to go up to the Small Plain tomorrow?"

His father nodded without looking up from his work.

"May I go along?"

"Of course, if you want to."

"Just look what a beautiful bridle I have now!" Jorge Gabriel proudly held up his handiwork.

"Splendid, splendid," said Don Gabriel. "Take it back now to the tack room."

"I will. Perhaps I can find another throatlatch."

Jorge Gabriel walked across the spacious patio, past the dining room where his mother sat doing needlework, past the rows of bedrooms, and then through the passage along the badly lit kitchens where the maids were still busy. He crossed the laundry patio, went past the ironing room and the servants' quarters, and then, stepping out through a little door, he faced the back row of utility buildings. It was dark there, and the household noises did not penetrate that far.

He walked by the machine room, the wooden chutes used to wash the coffee beans, the concrete drying floor. The horses were outside, the stalls were empty, yet the straw rustled. There was no shortage of rats here.

The door to the tool room stood open. The tack room, where sadles and harnesses hung in rows from the ceiling, was directly behind it. He smelled the odor of leather. He was almost there. . . .

20

THE HUT OF
THE TERRIBLE DEATH

Step by step Pulga made his way forward. Slowly, almost without any feeling, he plodded on.

In the subdued moonlight he could see the high, impassable mountains. There was no light, no sign of life anywhere. But he had to find someone. He had to!

Pulga waded through the tall grass and dark bushes. His ankles got entangled in tough vines and surface roots. Wet branches and ferns scratched across his face like sharp fingers. He shivered. His shirt clung to his sweat-covered body, his knees began to wobble. Down the hillside he groped his way as fast as he could. Pointed rocks tore into his body, thorns dug through his flimsy clothes. Fireflies hovered in the brush like evil-glowing eyes. The shrill chirping of crickets filled the night. The sound of rushing water from the river in the valley below mingled with the eerie whistling of the wind along the sides of the mountain. Everywhere the hellish music rose up from the brooding darkness.

Farther down, toward the river. . . . That was what Gilimon had said.

Pulga's feet sank into the soft ground. The chilly plants, the moist grass, the rotting soil seemed to suck him in. Silently he beat about lost in the moonlit landscape.

What was that? Did he hear something? A sound, steps . . . something! He listened, holding his breath. The wind blew through the bushes. Shadows swayed to and fro.

Was someone coming? Should he call out? But who would . . . at this time of night? Instinctively he crouched between the bushes, hidden under the leaves.

He listened, but heard nothing. The sound of crickets pierced the choking, green stillness. The phosphorescent lights of fireflies glowed above the underbrush. Was it the crickets? The fireflies? Or was it the whistling breath of the Madre Monte . . .

the sputtering light of La Candileja, seeking lost souls?

There it was again, the rustling between the bushes! Now . . . now the black wrap of the Madre Monte, with the chill of fog, would envelop him. Now. . . . He crouched, petrified, waiting . . . just waiting.

Branches moved; leaves shifted and touched him. The night was full of lisping sounds, of whispering voices. "Is this going to last much longer?"

Had he said that? Had he spoken out loud? There again . . . voices, soft, barely heard.

"They must be there now."

"Yes."

"It certainly takes a long time!"

"Till they get hold of the boy. . . ."

"I don't like any of this. . . . The whole plan. What are we going to do with the boy? And then when will we get the money?"

"Are you afraid?"

"Afraid! I just don't like it. Let me tell you. . . ."

"Just make sure the boss doesn't hear you."

"What of it?"

Then, several feet away from where Pulga was crouched, someone struck a match. In the light of the weak, little flame he could see the remnants of four collapsed walls, the last remainders of a miserable hut; the roof had disappeared long since.

The light of the moon sifted through the rotting beams. Plants and shrubs grew through the gaping openings. Where once the door had been, a man was standing with his back against a post, a gun resting horizontally in the crook of his arm. On the ground, in the thick growth of weeds, sat several other men dressed in dirty uniforms. Some wore boots, others loafers; some were barefoot. All were armed.

One of the men slowly lit a cigarette. He had hollow cheeks under deep-set eyes, and there was a cynical expression around his mouth.

"Watch it!"

"What for?"

"Watch out with that light. Somebody might see it."

"Come on now!" The words were said in a sneering tone of voice. "And suppose somebody does see it? Do you think he would come up here, at this hour, to this place?"

Another man answered. "Nobody has the guts to come here, not even in broad daylight. Sombra Negra has it all figured out. Our leader is not dumb, you know. No one has the courage to show up in these parts even if his life depends on it. They call it El Rancho de la Mala Muerte, the Hut of the Terrible Death. Well, it may well work out that way." The speaker laughed under his breath.

Pulga winced. The Hut of the Terrible Death! Sombra Negra! Good God, he thought, what have I gotten into? How am I going to get out of this? He sat there not daring to move.

The bandits were separated from him by a few bushes, some green leaves, and a crumbling wall. In the white light of the moon he could make out individual figures now, their faces hard, uncaring.

"If you ask me, it would have been better for the whole gang to stick together, the way we've always done. We would have handled anyone barring the way, and then taken what was worth it." The man who had spoken was sitting on the ground, his shoulder leaning against a collapsed wall. By stretching out his hand Pulga could have touched him.

"And what would we get that way?" asked another. "You know as well as the rest of us that those rich bastards don't keep a cent at the haciendas anymore. Sombra Negra thinks that a ransom will get us much more. It's a smart trick. He thinks—"

"He thinks, he thinks," snorted the other fellow. "And I tell you that nothing will come of it. Something is not right tonight. I just don't like it." With the butt of his gun he beat down on the bushes.

A loud shout broke the silence of the night.

The man on guard came to attention instantly. "Hold your tongue!" he ordered.

The men in the hut rose and took up their rifles. Once again they heard the same shout.

"All right, it's the boss," said the man on watch. The others relaxed. But Pulga sat tense and cramped under the huge leaves, wishing he could make himself even smaller. His whole body shivered. Those gun-butt blows had come down right next to his body. They had missed him by a hair's breadth. Petrified, he crouched even closer to the ground.

From among the bushes two men appeared carrying something heavy, wrapped in burlap. Noiselessly they walked over to the hut, where the men moved aside to make room for them. They saluted.

"*Mi capitán,*" they mumbled.

"Everything is fine," said Sombra Negra. He placed his end of the burden on the ground inside the hut among the weeds. One after another he looked his men over. He appeared to be younger and more intelligent than the rest. An arrogant grin seemed to be permanently engraved on his cruel mouth. "So there you have him," he said.

"It worked like a dream," said the man who had arrived with Sombra Negra. "He just walked into the trap."

"Take that bag off his head and give him something to drink," ordered Sombra Negra.

By now Pulga had managed to pull himself together. His curiosity had overcome his fear. Cautiously he stretched his neck and peered out between the leaves. With startled eyes he stared at the motionless figure lying on the ground.

There in the weeds lay a boy about Pulga's age. His hands and feet were bound, and on his forehead were streaks of clotted blood. He lay still as death, unconscious, hardly breathing.

"Pour some water over his face and put a bandage on his head." Sombra Negra watched to make sure that his order was carried out quickly and carefully. "And now, out! All of you. Let him alone till he comes to. He's worth his weight in gold."

Sombra Negra stepped out. The other men, muttering in agreement, shuffled after him.

That was the moment for Pulga to slither away.

21

PULGA'S STORY

The little village nestling against the side of the mountain was still wide awake. Men wrapped in their *ruanas*, with a *carriel*, a bag made of cowhide, slung over their shoulders, and a machete dangling from their hips, stood around in small groups outside the village inn. Children played in the steep climbing streets. Women sat on high doorsteps exchanging the day's gossip.

The marketplace, the only level piece of ground in the entire village, was bathed in moonlight. The blue, pink, and yellow houses clung to the mountainside like swallows' nests. The little balconies, jutting out from the tall, narrow houses seemed to be suspended in air.

The mayor was lying in his hammock on a balcony in back of his store. One of his legs hung over the edge of the hammock; his foot wiggled constantly. Over the low wooden bannister he could look out over the valley and the mountains. In the soft moonlight, the landscape appeared friendly and serene.

"Peaceful, isn't it," said the mayor.

"Yes, very peaceful," agreed his secretary, who was sitting next to him on a straight chair.

"Pour me another, please, and one for yourself."

Complying eagerly, the secretary poured two glasses of rum. The mayor let his flow down his throat in a single draught. He wiped his thick lips and repeated, "It really is peaceful."

At that moment somebody knocked at the door. The mayor turned his head in the direction of the kitchen and called, "Marcelina, somebody's at the door. Tell him the store is closed. Everything else can be taken care of tomorrow at my office." He sighed deeply. "You can't keep going all the time," he said to his secretary. "People here seem to think I have time for them day and night."

"That's the way it is," confirmed his secretary. "Would you care for another?"

Marcelina came shuffling in. "It's Pedro Rojas. You know, the one who drives the yellow pickup for the Public Works Department."

The mayor motioned impatiently. "Tomorrow, tomorrow I said."

"He's not alone," said Marcelina.

"Who's with him?"

"I wouldn't know. There are two of them, and they're not from around here. They want to talk to you, and they can't wait till tomorrow."

The mayor sat up. Pedro Rojas with the Public Works' pickup and two strangers. Who knows? They might be gentlemen from the Ministry in Bogotá. With his secretary close behind, the mayor walked swiftly through his store, which smelled of coffee and *panela* and rum, out to the front door.

There stood Gilimon and Pulga. Pedro Rojas, whose pickup had supplied the power to pull Gilimon's truck out of the ditch, stood behind them and whispered, "That's him. That's our mayor himself and his secretary." He hastily took off his sweat-drenched hat.

The mayor's face fell. Clearly these gentlemen were not from the Ministry in Bogotá. "What can I do for you?" he asked without any interest.

Gilimon pushed Pulga forward. "Tell your story, Pulga," he ordered.

Pulga's Story

Pulga shifted his bare feet in the dust and sand and said nothing.

"The thing is this," Gilimon finally said. "We had some trouble with the truck. The wheels slipped into the ditch. And then I sent my assistant down to get help. Well, when he came back we had the truck on the road, pulled it out with the pickup. It was luck that *Señor* Rojas came along. But my assistant was badly upset. He said . . . he claims, you see. . . . The story is a bit mixed up. He can tell you better himself."

With a look of disgust, the mayor examined the dirty little boy standing in front of him. To make matters worse, he stank. The mayor took a step back. "Well now, speak up. What have you got to tell me that's so important it can't wait till tomorrow morning?"

"They practically beat me to death," said Pulga.

"And for that you come and disturb me? That's nerve, I must say. They certainly didn't go after you for nothing. Let's have it. What were you doing?"

"I did nothing. . . ."

"Of course, of course. Your sort never does anything."

"I . . . I just tried to get downhill, to the river to get help, the way my boss told me to." Pulga meekly tried to defend himself. "But it was slow work. It

was so dark, and I didn't know the road, and then
. . . then I got to that house. . . ."

"To what house?"

"El Rancho de la Mala Muerte, the Hut of the Terrible Death, they called it."

"And who are 'they'?" asked the mayor sarcastically.

"The . . . the men who were sitting there."

"Were they the ones who almost beat you to death?"

Pulga nodded, relieved. "Yes, that's the way it was," he said.

The mayor turned to Gilimon and spoke sharply, "I understand that boy is yours, that is, your helper on your truck. Well, if I were in your shoes, I wouldn't let him fool me that easily. It's quite likely that he sat waiting in the bushes till the pickup came along. Let me tell you something: the Hut of the Terrible Death is a place where no mortal dares to go. I don't even know whether the hut is still there, or whether as much as a wall of it can be found. One thing I do know: a curse lies on that place. Everyone who ever lived there came to a bad end. No one has enough courage to go there, not even in full daylight. And that is where this helper of yours claims to have run into people."

The mayor laughed sneeringly and turned to Pulga. "What were the men doing there?"

"I . . . I didn't see him too well. He was lying out there among the weeds, and they had him tied up, and his head was covered with a piece of burlap. . . ." Pulga broke off, swallowed, and did not go on. Discouraged, he slumped his head down. How could he explain to these people what he had been through? They would not believe him.

The mayor turned angrily to Gilimon. "I don't know what this snot nose of yours has in mind," he said sharply. "But he's as full of lies as a stray dog is of fleas. First of all, no one would go anywhere near the Rancho de la Mala Muerte, and besides, this area is well guarded. A little farther up by the bridge an army detachment is stationed. And thirdly, if a boy were missing anywhere around here, we would have been informed long ago. My police setup functions flawlessly. I suppose this little monkey thought he could make all of us lose our heads and get excited. Perhaps he even thought he might get some money out of us." He looked contemptuously down at Pulga. "That's what you had in mind, wasn't it? But it's not going to work out that way, my little friend." He spat on the ground, right in front of Pulga's feet.

Pulga did not make the slightest effort to deny the truth of the mayor's insinuations. It would not have helped anyway. They simply refused to believe him. The mayor did not believe him, the secretary did not believe him, and Gilimon, it seemed, did not believe him either. He had looked very distrustful when Pulga had told him his story. Only the man with the yellow pickup was clearly shocked and shaken. He was the one who had insisted that they must go and see the mayor right away and had driven ahead to guide them to the village. Pulga looked stealthily around to make sure the pickup man had not left.

Meanwhile, outside the store entrance a crowd of people had gathered. They peered inside, nudged one another, and whispered.

"What's going on here?"

"I think one of those fellows there got caught."

"What did he do?"

"I don't know. He belongs to Sombra Negra's gang, I believe."

"Is that him? The little one there?"

"As far as I know. And the other one too, I think."

The news spread like wildfire. More people arrived, and the crowd outside the mayor's store kept growing larger. The mumbled, disconnected bits of conversation began to change to a threatening grumble. Pulga felt more and more uncomfortable. He tried to stay close to Gilimon. Needing help, he looked up to his boss.

"That's what you get for it, you ass," said Gilimon angrily. "What if they decide to detain us? It will give them a fine chance to ransack my truck." He looked anxiously across the square to where his damaged truck was standing.

"We ought to put that little rabble-rouser behind bars for a night," suggested the secretary.

"That's an excellent idea," the mayor said approvingly. "I haven't heard you say anything as bright as that in a long time." He glanced at the mob outside. "Look, he's managed to get my whole village excited, the little scoundrel." He turned away in disgust.

"Do you want me to have the officer on duty notified?" asked the secretary in a sudden burst of efficiency. "Call the officer on duty!" he shouted, without addressing anyone in particular.

"There he is! He's coming!" shouted some voices from farther back in the aroused crowd. "There comes the officer on duty! That's what I call quick service! Make room for him!"

"What's going on?"

"He's coming this way."

The crowd kept pushing. Nobody wanted to miss any part of the excitement.

"Step aside, out of the way!"

The officer on duty forced his way through the crowd. "Mayor!" he shouted at the retreating back of the mayor. "I received word just now—by phone,

I mean. The connection was very poor, and I couldn't understand everything. But I did make out . . . they said. . . . O my God, there they come, Ave María!"

Riders on sweating horses came galloping around the corner of the village square, straight up to the mayor's shop as the crowd made way.

"They're from La Virginia! There's Alejandro!"

The men jumped off their horses. Alejandro shouted, "Don Gabriel's son is missing. Yes, the boy —Jorge Gabriel!"

As though struck by a bolt of lightning the mayor turned around. "What!" he roared.

"The son of Don Gabriel of La Virginia is missing! The only son," Alejandro added. He was still out of breath, but he spoke clearly and distinctly. "He was on his way to the stable. The maids in the kitchen saw him passing by. When he did not return in a reasonable time, his father went to see what was going on. But the boy could not be found anywhere. Everybody at La Virginia has joined the search. We've gone over the entire plantation. But he's gone. He's been kidnapped, that much is certain. Sometime this afternoon I saw two men walk through the plantation. I told the boss about them when I reported to him tonight. Those men were strangers. . . ."

"Strangers," the mayor repeated hoarsely. "The

Pulga's Story

son of Don Gabriel of La Virginia kidnapped. . . . But in that case. . . ."

He cast a fierce look at his secretary. "Then the story that little brat told us is true! And you were standing there making fun of what he said, and to top it all you were ready to stick him in jail overnight. Where's the boy? He saw the whole thing. He can give us all the information we want on Sombra Negra's gang and the son of Don Gabriel. Don't just stand there looking like a born fool! Go find the boy and the driver, too, and bring them here. Hurry!"

Terrified, the secretary looked around frantically, then ran across to the square. "Where's the boy? Where's the driver?" he shouted at no one in particular as he pushed through the crowd. "Help me look! Help me look! Where's the truck?"

But the truck was gone. Gilimon and Pulga had taken advantage of the confusion to slip away. By now they were well on the road.

22

THE ACCIDENT

"Well done, outstandingly well done, mayor," said Don Gabriel.

The mayor raised his fat hand as though to ward off excess appreciation. "Not at all, always glad to be of service," he said humbly.

But Don Gabriel hardly listened. Softly he continued, "My wife, and myself, we cannot thank you enough. Our boy...." Don Gabriel turned halfway around toward Jorge Gabriel's room. He heard the light tread of his wife, who was at the bedside of their son. Gently she was bathing his face and rub-

The Accident

bing his wrists where the ropes had left painful welts.

Don Gabriel swallowed. "Well done, outstandingly well done," he repeated to the mayor. "I . . . I dare not think of what could have happened, of what they might have done to him. You know that we found a threatening letter not far from the stable, a letter mentioning an enormous ransom. I am not a poor man, but where could I find such a sum in so short a time? And then, what happens meanwhile to the child? Those bandits know no mercy. . . ."

"That's right," answered the mayor, "they know no mercy. They are wild beasts. The way they fought down there, by the Rancho de la Mala Muerte. But we had them surrounded on all sides. It's a pity Sombra Negra got away. Anyway most of them are accounted for. Dead or alive, the gang no longer exists, that we can say." The mayor spoke without trying to hide his pride.

"Yes, it was a neat job. Unheard of, incredible the way the soldiers and the police from your village lost no time rounding them up."

Modestly, the mayor did not reply.

Don Gabriel waited a few moments. Then he said, "I understand that you got a tip from somewhere. The details are not quite clear to me. Was the person actually there?"

"Yes," conceded the mayor. "That's what happened, roughly speaking. Oh, well, let's put it this way: without a bit of luck, where would one be?" He laughed lightly.

"Yes, that's true. Still, I would like to know a little more," Don Gabriel said. "If I didn't get the story all wrong, there was a boy who told you where the hideout of the bandits was. A . . . a poor boy, I understand. I would like"—Don Gabriel cleared his throat—"I would like to do something for that boy. Set aside a sum of money or find him a job or pay his way through school . . . something like that. Something that would last throughout the remainder of his life. I am sure you know what I mean."

"Yes, indeed," said the mayor. "I do, I understand what you mean."

"If you will let me have the boy's name and his present address. . . ."

For a moment the mayor looked startled. "Well," he said hesitantly. "Perhaps, though, it won't be quite that easy. I. . . ."

"But surely you took down his name and address when he came to give you the information," said Don Gabriel rather impatiently. "What could be difficult about copying his name and address from your files?"

"Of course, of course. . . ." said the mayor, trying to smooth over his blunder. "What I mean is that the name of the boy has slipped my mind. But I'm sure my secretary has recorded everything. I'll ask

The Accident

him right away . . . you'll certainly hear from him." The conversation had taken a highly unpleasant turn. Suddenly in a great hurry, the mayor got up and left. He climbed into his car and drove away.

The dirty little brat, what was his name? Where did he come from? What had become of him?

Impatiently the mayor shrugged off these bothersome questions. Didn't he have enough headaches? He was not going to lose a night's sleep over this nonsense.

As he sat by Gilimon's side, Pulga was unaware of the tight spot the mayor had maneuvered himself into, unaware of everything that had transpired at the Hut of the Terrible Death following their escape from the mayor's house. Vacantly he stared out the window. He felt beaten and deeply unhappy. But he did not want to think about the situation. Now he must have a clear head. He needed it as they delivered their refrigerators in the torrid little villages of the Magdalena valley. He was not going to make another mistake. Not one!

Gilimon was not in the best possible mood either. He had not uttered a word for some time. Pulga knew that his chance of getting hired for another trip was lost. There was no future for him as the helper on this truck.

Indeed, by a hair's breadth he had missed being

thrown in jail. Possibly Gilimon, too. If that had happened, the truck would have been robbed or impounded. They would have lost everything, and it would have been all his fault.

But where had things gone wrong? All of it was true . . . the bandits . . . the boy. . . . What should he have done that he had failed to do? He had tried so hard and had done his best to do things the way Gilimon wanted them done. He had tried so hard to show that he was somebody.

Not long ago—not even two weeks—he had caught a glimpse of another life. He had found a goal. He had found someone he belonged to. Gilimon had taken him along in his big shining truck. That had been his chance.

In the deepest part of his being he had been aware of that, aware deep down where life is concerned with self-preservation and nothing else. He had seized that chance, grabbed it with the desperate strength of a starved animal. He had worked. He had looked after the truck, done his very best. He had been the boss's helper . . . faithful . . . unfailing. He had hoped so much that he might stay with Gilimon . . . continue to be his helper on the truck. Vaguely he knew that he had played with still more ambitious plans. To learn something about a motor, possibly to learn how to drive, and perhaps someday. . . . For a while

The Accident

his future had seemed to lie in his hands. That was no longer true, not anymore.

What could he do about it? Pulga bit his lips. Don't think. Don't argue. Watch out! Do your work! No more blunders!

Over the horizon, over the sweltering plain, they approached their next stopping place, the small town of Girardot on the Magdalena River. There they drove across the bridge, through the narrow streets to the freight office, and from there to the store where the refrigerators were to be delivered. Pulga's every nerve was tensed as he gave his utmost attention to each detail of his job. He looked for and found the man with whom they had to deal. He saw that the right number of refrigerators was unloaded. He made sure the bills of lading were signed. Once again he checked the remaining load that had to be taken to Bogotá. He cleaned the windshield and side windows of the cab. He watched like an eagle while the gas tank and the radiator were filled. He kept a sharp eye on everything.

Finally they were ready to drive on. The last stretch of their trip back to Bogotá had begun.

The road was climbing. They drove across the Boquerón, a narrow pass, where the rushing waters of a swift river had cut a gorge into the rock. The road beside it was winding and narrow. Where it widened again, there were small fruit stands and roadside restaurants.

Gilimon pulled up in front of one of the restaurants and went up onto the porch, looking for a place to sit down in the shade. Pulga followed him silently, carrying, as always, Gilimon's suitcase under his arm.

"Gilimo-o-o-n, what a pleasure. . . . Gilimo-o-o-n!" Polidorio rose from his chair at one of the little tables. "Gilimo-o-o-n, over here! Come and sit with me."

Gilimon's face lit up. "Polidorio! What a miracle! How have things been? Did you have to hang around in Barranquilla for long?"

"Just one day—a whole day though—and in that heat. But we did have fun, didn't we? How did you make out? Did you manage to get a halfway decent consignment?"

"Cement to Montería and after that a load to Copacabana outside of Medellín."

"I see. Cattle, I guess."

"Right, cattle."

"I don't envy you. They can kick your truck to pieces. And when it comes time to pay, those cattlemen cling to their pennies."

"This time I did get a decent price."

"Your good luck! Come to think of it, my good

luck, too. That calls for a celebration, doesn't it?" He burst out in that familiar, roaring laughter. He wiped the sweat off his forehead and winked at Pulga. "And you, my boy. How goes it? Everything all right?"

Pulga nodded shyly.

"Say! Did you hear the latest? In Barranquilla they told me that that beanstalk Lauriano, who's always hanging around the ferry and can't keep his fingers out of other people's pockets, got bitten by a dog. By a dog . . . ha ha. . . ." He slapped his knees with pleasure and laughed heartily.

Pulga blushed and said nothing.

Gilimon ordered beer and something to eat.

"Coming from Medellín?" he asked Polidorio.

"That's it. And yesterday they stole my windshield wipers, those scoundrels. Well, there's always something in our line of work!" he said with a sigh, his huge belly heaving. "Anyway we're practically there. I'll be glad to be home for a spell." He shoved his glass away from the edge of the table and got up.

"So long now. We'll bump into each other again. And thanks for the beer."

"My pleasure," Gilimon said. "And lots of luck."

"The same to you."

"Best of luck!"

Polidorio left. Jolly and laughing, he walked across the veranda, exchanging greetings right and left.

Gilimon and Pulga gulped down their food and walked back to the truck. Just then a crowded bus came along in a cloud of dust and stopped outside the restaurant. A horde of people came pouring out of the bus. Pulga stopped and stood there as though he were nailed to the ground.

That man! That man with the haughty expression on his face, with his small supercilious laugh. Where had he seen him? Where had he seen that face?

Gilimon was sitting at the wheel already, impatiently honking his horn.

Pulga came to and quickly climbed in next to Gilimon. "Boss, you see that man there? That's him. . . ."

"Who?" Gilimon asked and looked outside.

"The man who just walked in through the door. That's him. That's Sombra Negra!"

Gilimon started the motor, shifted into low gear, and slowly the truck began to move. "If you ask me, you'll keep your trap shut," Gilimon said. "I'll be damned if I ever stick my nose in other people's business again. What a reception we got from that fathead of a mayor."

Leaving a cloud of dust behind, they swung back onto the main road. Soon the Boquerón was out of sight. As they climbed, the mountains of the eastern

The Accident

chain of the Andes closed in around them little by little, ever higher and more forbidding and hostile. Gradually the heat declined, the vegetation changed, and slowly the light withdrew from the earth. The clouds coming from the valley of the Magdalena River settled into long white stripes between the hazy mountaintops.

They kept climbing higher and higher into the mountains, among the bare, precipitous rocks, where they had to pass in order to reach the Sabana de Bogatá. Cars, buses, and trucks kept rolling along the narrow road in both directions. Trucks from Cali, Medellín, and Manizales going up, huge loads of iron from Paz del Río and goods from Bogatá coming down, headed toward Neiva or Cali or Buenaventura.

Beyond Fusa a drizzling rain began to fall and wet fog mingled with the falling darkness. Yellow headlights pierced the grayness all around them. The red and blue and green signal lights over the cab windows and around the vans looked like Christmas decorations. The narrow road, hewn out of sheer rock, grew still steeper. More and more cars fell out. They stood along the road with open hoods, their radiators steaming like sweating horses.

Gilimon's truck crept up the mighty mountain like a small brown beetle. The windshield wipers ticked monotonously. From time to time Pulga wiped the condensation off the glass. Gilimon's strong hands clasped the steering wheel, pulling the heavy vehicle around the sharp turns. Then, all of a sudden, he stopped.

A row of cars was lined up ahead. Drivers and passengers were standing at the outer edge of the road, looking down into the ravine. Gilimon and Pulga got out.

"There is someone lying down there," said a man.

In the long, wet grass were deep tire marks, leading down to the edge of the precipice . . . down into the ravine. Colorless trees rose up from below, and thin streaks of mist hovered among the treetops. A few broken branches were visible, but the dense vegetation closed off the everyday scene.

The people were standing close together along the edge of the road, looking down into the chasm, which sent up nothing but the rushing sound of a small river. Water trickled down the steep, gray wall of rock along the opposite side of the road. Heavy drops fell on the huge fern fronds by the roadside.

"It was a truck," said a tall youngster, standing near his dilapidated jeep.

Gilimon looked up. "Did you see it?" he asked.

The youth nodded. "It was awful."

A crowd of people gathered around him, including some who had heard the story several times.

"I saw it happen," he said emphatically. "He was

coming around the curve and wanted to clear that broken-down pickup over there. And then I saw him go down into the ravine . . . just like that."

"What kind of truck was it?" Gilimon asked.

The young man shrugged his shoulders. "Hard to say," he said. "It all happened so fast . . . and the fog. . . . I think I saw the front wheel slide off the road, and then the truck began to topple over and . . . and that was that . . . Ave María Bendita." He made the sign of the Cross.

The lines of vehicles along both sides of the road kept growing longer. Some of the people indulged in a guessing game. Maybe the driver saw the broken-down pickup too late. Maybe he was blinded by oncoming headlights. Maybe the brakes failed. Maybe he had fallen asleep. Truck drivers these days with their long trips. . . .

"What should we do?"

"Bogotá has been informed. A wrecking car should be on its way by now."

The young man who had seen it happen began once again, "It was a truck, a huge—"

"What color truck was it?" Gilimon interrupted.

Again the young fellow shrugged his shoulders. "Blue. Or perhaps green. . . . I don't know. It all happened so fast. . . ."

The drivers at the extreme ends of the two rows of cars began to honk their horns impatiently. The road was swarming with people standing around in groups, milling about aimlessly in the cold fog . . . insignificant in the vast darkness of the night.

With a movement of his head, Gilimon ordered Pulga to climb up into the cab. Slowly they drove along, following the car ahead and guiding the one behind. When they reached the smoke-blackened statue of the Virgin in a small niche in the rock wall, Gilimon stopped and climbed out. He lit a candle from the box at the shrine and placed it among the other flickering candles. His hand was unsteady. For a few moments he stood before the small statue of Mary.

Then they drove on.

23

HOMECOMING

The mountains opened up. The truck rolled along over the uplands plateau. Cold, moist air blew into the cab.

Gilimon pulled up in the dim light of a kerosene lamp outside a small restaurant. The place was full of cars, buses, and trucks. The accident was the sole topic of conversation.

Gilimon ordered a beer and kept to himself. For a long time he just sat, staring into a void. A little old man, struggling with a couple of bags full of moss and a couple of thin fir branches, stepped up to him.

"You're not going to Bogotá by any chance, *señor*? Could I possibly come with you. I've been standing here for a long, long time, but nobody seems to be willing to take me along. Most of the trucks are full, and here I stand with my moss and my trees. I've been told that foreigners in town pay a good price for a Christmas tree. I don't know, but why not try? Everybody has his own way of living, and it's quite possible that these foreigners will pay a good price to preserve their customs. I thought if I go to town tonight, then I'll be there early in the morning and ready with all my stuff. But nobody has room. I thought if I. . . ."

"All right," Gilimon said. "You can put your bags and your branches in the back of the truck and climb in yourself. There's room enough for you." Gilimon pushed his empty beer bottle away, paid, and got into the cab next to Pulga.

They were traveling rather fast now along the straight and smooth road. Everywhere across the land small lights were coming on. The mountain range along which Bogotá lies appeared in an ocean of twinkling lights.

Pulga sat quietly in his corner. He did not dare to ask about the accident and much less about the matter that preoccupied him more than anything else: what plans Gilimon had for him. Should he ask him to take him along again as his helper for the next trip?

Gilimon remained silent, and Pulga felt quite sure that his boss's thoughts were not concerned with him. What could one do? One has to accept life as it comes. Just like that.

As they neared the city, the familiar feeling of resigned submission took hold of Pulga. The paralyzing feeling that there simply was no way of changing things around. He had to accept what was coming to him without objection, without resistance. There were no two ways about that.

Finally Gilimon broke the silence. "The man back there on the truck has a couple of puny fir branches."

"Yes, I saw, too," Pulga answered. "Fir and moss, for Christmas. . . ."

Yes, of course, it was almost Christmas. Down in the hot country, he hadn't thought of it for even a moment. Now it all came back to him.

When Gilimon and he had started out, there were a few places in the city where people had already begun to put up Christmas decorations. By this time no doubt all the stores were decorated, and all the colorful neon lights were strung across the streets, displaying the inscription, *Merry Christmas.*

"Actually it isn't a bad idea," said Gilimon deep in thought. "Fir trees . . . at Mamá Maruja's there are lots of them. I really could. . . ."

Pulga's heart beat faster. Mamá Maruja! He hadn't thought about her for a long time.

Now that Gilimon had mentioned her name, he saw her suddenly. There she stood, strong and angular, a somberly dressed woman with work-toughened hands and a furrowed face, proud, not to be swayed, righteous. A deep desire arose in him to see her again . . . the small, quiet valley . . . to hear the rushing waterfall and the whistling sound of the wind in the fir trees.

"Yes," he said quickly, "there are a great many such trees there."

"Perhaps it might be worthwhile to drive to her place one day and get a load," Gilimon suggested. "A little something extra would be in it for Mamá Maruja, of course. She could use it. She's not as young as she used to be."

"Yes," Pulga agreed. He hesitated, now or never. "Yes, when we were at her place she said that she could use an extra pair of hands . . . a boy like me, for instance. . . . That is what she said." He held his breath and waited tensely.

There was no reaction. They were now in the city's busy streets, and the traffic claimed Gilimon's full attention. Slowly they turned into a narrow street full of trucks.

Pulga recognized the street.

The truck stopped. "Here we are," Gilimon said.

They climbed out of the cab and stood by the side of the huge truck covered with dust and mud. Together they had covered a distance of more than three thousand kilometers, and now there was little to be said.

"Here's your money, Pulga," said Gilimon. "So that's settled. And thank you, Pulga!"

Pulga accepted the money. Almost a hundred pesos. He did not put it in his pants' pocket; it wouldn't be safe there. He clutched the money in his fist and looked at Gilimon. Should he ask the question? Now? Just like that? He hesitated.

"Yes?" said Gilimon. "Is something wrong? Did you think you'd get more?"

Pulga shook his head.

"Well, what is it? You stand there and look. . . ."

"I wanted to ask you whether—"

"Gilimon!" A driver in a short leather jacket came hurrying toward them. "We just got the report. It was a truck of the Phoenix outfit."

"Polidorio," Gilimon said flatly.

The other man nodded. "Yes, Polidorio," he repeated.

Gilimon slowly turned away. Two heavy steps took him to the door of the cab. He climbed inside and slammed the door.

The man looked at Pulga. "I guess the news shook him up," he said.

"Yes," Pulga answered. "They were friends. . . . I knew him too."

"You belong with this truck?" asked the driver.

"Yes . . . no. . . ." Almost inaudibly Pulga added, "I've just been paid off."

The driver did not hear him. He walked away down the street. Pulga stood there staring after him. Suddenly the little old man came up to him.

"I'm sure I can leave the bags of moss and my Christmas trees on the truck till tomorrow morning," he said. "I'm going to see my son now, but he lives quite a distance away."

Pulga nodded absently. He clutched his money tighter in his hand. Slowly, without looking back, he left the street.

Farther along, in one of the busy, brightly lit shopping streets, where hawkers were standing along the sidewalk with clothing, foodstuffs, toys, and fireworks, Pulga did his shopping. A shirt for himself and for Pedro. Two plastic dolls for his sisters, and a bagful of sweet rolls—with icing on top—for his grandmother. He decided not to buy shoes for himself right now. He wanted to wait until he had more time. Finally he bought some sparklers and firecrackers that they all could enjoy. Imagine their faces when he suddenly appeared before their very noses, carrying all those beautiful gifts.

He walked faster. There was the street going uphill, and over there was the house. He walked through the chilly passageway across the patio. In Rose-Alba's little room he heard the whir of her sewing machine, and under the stairs the old shoemaker was at work by the light of a candle, his son beside him, a bottle within reach.

Everything was the way he had left it. Nothing had changed. He hurried down the hall, pushed open the door leading into the room, and stepped inside.

A woman who was busy unrolling mattresses on the floor looked up. "What do you want here?" she asked.

"I . . ." Pulga looked around.

A flock of children played among the mattresses. In the far corner stood the bed.

"I live here," said Pulga.

The woman stood up, pushed back some strands of stray hair behind her ears, and firmly placed her hands on her hips. "What? What are you trying to tell me?"

"I live here," Pulga repeated. He pointed to the bed. "That bed is ours. I. . . ."

"You live here, you live here," said the woman,

mimicking his voice. "Get out! Vanish, you dirty rascal! It's not enough that ten of us must sleep here on the floor, and now you plan to pull the bed out from under me! Out, and make it fast!" She stepped across the mattresses toward Pulga.

Slowly he moved back out of the room. He stood outside in the patio, holding his gifts tightly.

From her storage room, Eulalia-with-the-Ear had been watching him attentively. When the woman had slammed her door shut, Eulalia came out and peered at Pulga. "Are you looking for your grandmother?" she asked.

Pulga nodded.

"She isn't around any longer."

"But then, where is she?"

"She is dead."

"Dead," Pulga repeated. "And my sisters . . . and Pedro. . . ?"

"Your sisters?" She shrugged her shoulders. "Who knows? I think they were taken to some home."

"And . . . and Pedro?"

"Pedro . . . the cripple. . . . I haven't seen him for quite a while either, now that you mention it. He's gone."

"Gone? Where to? Where can I. . . ?"

Again Eulalia-with-the-Ear shrugged her shoulders. "Who knows? He's gone."

Clasping his packages to his body, Pulga stood there in the center of the patio, staring vacantly at Eulalia. What was he to do now? His grandmother was dead. Other people were living in the room that had been his home. His sisters were in an orphanage . . . or somewhere. And Pedro . . . ? He must find Pedro.

Eulalia-with-the-Ear watched him silently.

Slowly Pulga walked in the direction of the passageway and the street. His bag of sweet rolls slipped from under his arm and fell on the ground unnoticed. When he was safely out of sight, the old woman shuffled over to where the bag lay, snatched it up, and went back into her storage room. She looked rather pleased.

Pulga first went to Tío Pepe. But that visit proved to be a waste of time. Tío Pepe called Pedro an ingrate who had sneaked away without as much as a word of thanks. Tío Pepe had written him off. He had nothing more to say to Pedro, and less to Pulga.

Without waiting for him to finish his harangue, Pulga left and headed in the direction of the center of town. He walked past the movie theaters and asked the boys he knew if they had seen his little brother.

"Pedro?" They shrugged their shoulders. Why should they care?

Finally one of the boys remarked, "You mean the cripple? The one with a foot screwed on the wrong way?"

Pulga nodded. "Yes, that's the one. . . ."

"I saw him just a few days ago slipping through a hole in the wooden fence," the boy said. "You know, the fence around the building lot, down there at the corner. But whether he's still there is hard to say."

Pulga walked as fast as the traffic permitted down the broad shopping street where red and green Christmas advertisements kept flicking on and off, on and off. . . . Over there, in the dark section of the street, was the fence. He looked around quickly, then slipped through the opening between two loose boards.

It was dark in the empty lot, and the city noises were muted. Pulga stood in a clump of rank weeds. The soil smelled sour.

Cautiously he made his way over the uneven ground. "Pedro!" he called out.

There was no answer. He stopped and listened. Over there by the wall of the building he heard a rustling noise. He ran as fast as he could, calling, "Pedro, Pedro!"

From between some boards that were leaning against the wall, a scrawny figure emerged, a small, scared boy with frightened eyes. He stood with his back against the wall. Red and green lights of Christmas advertisements flickered over him.

"What do you want?" he said.

"Pedro!"

"What do you want? I didn't do anything."

"Pedro! It's me—Pulga! I've come to take you with me."

"Take me with you?" Slowly, a step at a time, he came toward Pulga. "Come to take me with you," he repeated. "Where . . . where are we going?"

"We're going. . . ." Pulga hesitated. Then he took his brother's hand and dragged Pedro behind him. "Come along," he said.

They walked through the city that was all dressed up in its Christmas finery, along the busy streets, past the brightly lit stores. They had to force their way through the crowds.

After a while the streets became quieter and darker. They turned a corner, and there stood the truck. There, in the cab, sat Gilimon staring.

Pulga tapped on the window.

Gilimon, startled out of his daze, looked outside and saw two small, weary faces. Slowly he stepped down from the cab. "Pulga, what are you doing here? I thought you had gone home long ago. And who is that, in God's name?"

"Pedro."

"Is this your little brother?"

Pulga nodded.

"And what is it you want?"

"We want to go with you to Mamá Maruja," said Pulga. "Pedro can stay with her and help her. And I—"

"Now I get it," said Gilimon. "For yourself, you want to be hired for good as the helper on my truck. Well, I think I'll let that simmer till tomorrow morning. Just make sure that you're here tomorrow morning at half. . . ."

Pulga did not wait to hear the rest. He pulled Pedro along with him to the rear of the truck. Together they climbed in. They could go to Mamá Maruja, perhaps tomorrow. And Pedro could stay there and help her. Then he and Gilimon. . . .

They fell asleep on the moss among the Christmas trees.